THE DOUBTFUL DISCIPLE

Charles Russell, of the Security Executive, was getting no younger and knew that the time had come to assume the role of an *éminence grise*. So Richard Laver was promoted, to his own surprise, and this was his first case—'a typical one to start you on', said Russell's covering note on the file.

It concerned S.P.D.—Selective Pigmentation Disease—something particularly nasty which had been produced by the Chemical Defence Experimental Establishment in Wiltshire. A development of biological warfare which overcame the distressing probability that the aggressor might suffer the disease he unleashed on his brothers—or would do so if they happened to be of a different colour. And now there was the possibility of a major leak. The key, it appeared, was Mervin Seyer, a brilliant scientist concerned with S.P.D., whose mind was going as the result of a serious car accident. Seyer had frantically turned to religion and was on the Committee supporting Jacky D, a rabid evangelist. And when two events occurred in quick succession to discredit Jacky D and make him vulnerable, Laver became convinced that the connection between him and the ailing geneticist was a great deal more sinister than one of master and disciple.

With all the tenacity which marked the former Head of Security Executive, Laver pursues the tenuous clues, apparently getting nowhere and always waiting anxiously for the penny to drop. Which it does, in a sudden climax, in Amsterdam.

WILLIAM HAGGARD

THE DOUBTFUL DISCIPLE

CASSELL · LONDON

CASSELL & COMPANY LTD
35 Red Lion Square, London WC1
Melbourne, Sydney, Toronto
Johannesburg, Auckland

© William Haggard 1969
First published 1969

S.B.N. 304 93287 6

Printed in Great Britain
by Ebenezer Baylis & Son, Ltd
The Trinity Press, Worcester, and
London
F. 469

1

Richard Laver was finding his first day in the Security Executive very much as was any first day in a brand-new job, and as a civil servant of what was absurdly called the Administrative Grade he had had experience of many. There was a tradition that the gifted amateur, the man with a First Class degree from Oxbridge, could handle anything new of his own sole virtue, and though this had slightly faded of late the extent of the fade wasn't noticeable to the other grades. Just the same, he had never expected the Executive.

And at forty-five not very much else. He was an Under-Secretary and would stick there now, a respectable rank and even what was called senior, but well below his real potential. He knew he was able and to the best of his knowledge he'd never achieved a serious clanger, but men junior to him had been promoted, and though it hadn't soured him he'd made his guesses. Perhaps it was Mary, the wife he was devoted to. She wrote successful romantic novels which made her a good deal of money, they had a comfortable house in Provost Road and a cottage in the country. Richard himself had an ageing R-Type Bentley, so perhaps, he'd thought, his smell had been wrong, the wrong sort of aura for the last of the nineteen-sixties. It was rubbish of course, and it had also annoyed him. As though an official worked any the less efficiently for the fact that he lived in a civilized way. But alas there were men to resent it—asses.

The summons to Number Ten had knocked him flat. Under-Secretaries weren't called to the Prime Minister's house, or only, and that very rarely indeed, through the most official of official channels. Experienced, careful of protocol, Richard Laver had told his Permanent Secretary, but Sir Henry had urged him to go at once. He'd implied that he wasn't surprised at the call but that Laver could well be surprised at its purpose.

He was thinking now that indeed he had been, even more so at the Prime Minister's manner. He had never put a foot wrong from first to last. . . . And how was Mrs. Laver? Well, he trusted. He read her books avidly since he liked a good read. In the Prime Minister's opinion they were a great deal better written than many more serious novels which the heavies reviewed as literature, and in any case fiction was entertainment. If you wanted a dose of sociology you should take it from a Blue Book with facts and figures. Perhaps that was square? Then the Prime Minister was square as hell. . . . And Laver's son Robert—a merchant bank, wasn't it? (Yes, he'd read Laver's file and much besides.) Doing well, very steady. As for Patty, she'd settle down, no doubt. Richard Laver wasn't alone in that, the Prime Minister had a daughter too and she kept him and his wife awake at night. Just the same a wild daughter wasn't wholly a liability since she kept one in touch with people whom otherwise . . . If Charles Russell had had a defect it was simply that he was a bachelor.

It had dawned on Laver incredulously that he was going to be offered Charles Russell's job, indeed the Prime Minister, oblique as ever, was reciting his qualification before the Executive had even been named. . . . Richard Laver was an official but he was something more than a typical one; he had fought in a war with distinction too, and the Staff College had thought well of him. That didn't happen to narrow men unless they were also professional soldiers. A narrow man—that would be fatal. But Laver had interests outside his work and it was known he wasn't begging a little butter to whet his bread. That was important since the worst man for the Executive would be the breakneck careerist so many were. So perhaps he was wondering why he hadn't gone further. A legitimate question though never asked and

2

the Prime Minister would now answer it. A decision of this sort wasn't taken on the nail, indeed it had been made three years and a little more ago. Laver had been earmarked for the Security Executive the moment Charles Russell had made it clear that he didn't intend to serve beyond sixty, or rather that at sixty-one he didn't propose to come in every day. He'd be around for many more years, he hoped, and he'd always be available, but the time had come to go *éminence grise*, to let a younger man handle the routine work.

Laver had found himself hoping passionately that the Prime Minister wouldn't boob it now. He had met Charles Russell and much admired him, though he wasn't his personal cup of tea, but a Prime Minister of this one's party could succumb to temptation and knock Russell cruelly— the man's unashamed and quite genuine upper crustiness, his taste for field sports, his stuffy old club. But the Prime Minister did none of this: instead he said simply that Russell was irreplaceable and that it was no denigration of Richard Laver to say he'd do well if he filled his chair.

And why had he been selected since except for the last years of a war he'd never been in Intelligence? Again a legitimate question and one even harder to answer. The Prime Minister puffed a disgusting pipe. Let him put it as a negative since the positive eluded him. There was an organization for catching spies, and though it had had its notorious failures it had also had secret successes which few men knew. A man needed one sort of technique for that but something quite different to be Head of the Executive. The Security Executive seldom caught spies directly, and then only by invitation of other bodies. Its work was on the penumbra of politics, the fact, for instance (and why conceal it?) that more than one member of the Prime Minister's own party was secretly committed to a totally alien government. And for that sort of work one needed a flair, flair and discretion, above all things a private ethos. That was essential but how was he to put it? It was really rather difficult, but it wasn't so very long ago that the smell of success in Whitehall had been sharply definable: an orthodox liberal humanism or you didn't get very far up the ladder. But by now that didn't go at all. How to put it again? He'd have a shot. Laver was here because he'd quietly despaired and all first class men had long since despaired. The world was too complex for anything else, the old labels of Left and Right quite meaningless except as differing styles for the same dread thing, the staving off total disaster if that could be done.

Mr. Laver agreed? Then Mr. Laver was in. The salary was eight, by the way, and the pension wouldn't be less than four. It wasn't published in any official book, and by God the incumbent earned it.

So Laver sat quietly in Russell's chair and he was feeling extremely lonely. There had been no sort of formal hand-over for Charles Russell didn't believe in them. He'd be available as he'd said he would and perhaps he could still be useful, but he wouldn't come in daily to some comfortably carpeted room at the back nor accept some ridiculous title as Lord Adviser. They could come to him still and he hoped they would, but he wouldn't sit reading the newspapers. The way to learn to drive a car, or a railway train or to shoot a gun was to go out and buy a car or a train, or a shotgun which properly fitted you.

Richard Laver had laughed at the time but not now. He looked at the file on his desk which was marked TOP SECRET. The Executive over-graded seldom, so that meant it was very hot indeed.

> TOP SECRET (S.E. 124/1969)
> S.P.D.
> (Selective Pigmentation Disease?)

4

Inside was one of Charles Russell's Minutes:

Quite a typical case to start you on. Nothing concrete to go on, but the possibility of a major leak. Dominy has been down to Wiltshire to poke about. I have told him to speak to you.

Laver sent for Martin Dominy, an ex-operator promoted to chief assistant. Laver, quite new, was grateful for Russell's lead.

Martin Dominy came in quietly, standing till he was asked to sit. Then Laver said conversationally:

'So you've been poking about in Wiltshire.'

'And they're on to something new, I think. We've had the standard official denials for months and years, but if anyone took them seriously they'd have to believe that place was maintained for fun. No, they've got something new.'

'What sort of something? Chemical warfare or micro-biological?'

'They didn't tell me, naturally. But I doubt if it's chemical warfare.'

Laver asked sharply: 'Why do you doubt?'

Martin Dominy shrugged. 'Why should it be chemical warfare? That side of the Establishment has got about as far as it can go. Rather like the Bomb, in fact. A sort of balance of terror.'

Richard Laver was silent—he shared the guess. There was a great deal of talk about biological warfare, a great deal of naked fear which he shared himself, but when you looked at it dispassionately it was still a second best—you hoped. There were a dozen chemical hellbrews which would wreck the world much quicker, organo-phosphorous compounds and their successors in shameful title. The nerve gases, so called, for one. They were easier to make than some delicate micro-organism; they couldn't backlash home on you if the hideous infection spread; above all they were much simpler to deliver. Who would happily risk some new plague abroad when he had only the Channel to guard himself? A few miles of sea or a programme of mass inoculation of your own people, which was the sort of thing you could never keep hidden, expense aside. No sensible strategist would risk it when he had *Tabrun* freely available, and that horror by now was almost old-fashioned. So germ warfare was still a second best, a very uncertain second at that.

Once again you despairingly hoped so.

That was the position, for what cold comfort it was worth. That was the position, or rather it seemed it might have been. Richard Laver sighed softly. 'You really think they've got something new?'

'If I were a betting man I'd bet.'

'But what good would it do them? There are plenty already—Rocky Mountain fever, Tulataemia, Coccidiodo-mycosis, the whole catalogue of hell. And you know the disadvantages just as well as I do. Germs aren't nationality-conscious, germs don't ask to see people's passports.'

'They haven't so far,' Dominy said.

'*What was that?*'

'I wish I knew, but there's certainly something brewing.' Martin Dominy reflected. 'Have you heard of Mervin Seyer?'

'Of course I have. My wife's maternal grandmother's sister married his grandfather.' Laver reflected in turn. He had married a Scot and was careful of relationships. 'That makes us second cousins by marriage. It isn't really important since in practice I hardly know him, but I know his daughter Margaret since an aunt of hers asked for our interest. Not that it was necessary in any way at all. She's a very attractive woman but knows perfectly how to take care of herself. But there's something about her . . .'

He left it unfinished but thought instead. Margaret Seyer stood out in a crowd of women but if she'd been a man he'd have called her tough. Also he'd heard on the family grape-vine that a coloured man was courting her. Well, she could handle that and much else besides. A dying father, for instance—she was managing that superbly. He looked up again at Dominy who seemed to expect some further comment. Laver didn't offer it but he added a little elliptically:

'A man would have to be very sure. Be that as it may, Margaret Seyer and I are second cousins once removed. She has been known to call me uncle but I don't feel I'm nearly old enough for the insult.'

Martin Dominy ignored all this. 'Mervin Seyer has broken up, you know.'

'I do. But he was seventy and a bit, I'd guess, and that car smash he had was pretty bad.'

'You don't think his work in Wiltshire broke him?'

'It might have been a factor, of course. He had a highly developed social conscience, and that isn't an easy bedfellow when your work could murder millions of men.'

Dominy let this pass again. 'But what was he doing in Wiltshire at all?'

'He's a scientist, isn't he?'

'Yes, but he isn't a chemist, nor a microbiologist either. He's a geneticist, one of the world's top dozen.'

'And so?'

Dominy said thoughtfully: 'You were talking about germs not asking to see people's passports; they aren't, you said, race-conscious.' He leant forward deliberately. 'They don't notice the colour of people's skins. *Or rather they haven't so far.*'

There was a protracted, a stricken silence. Laver said at the end of it, his voice almost toneless: 'They told you that was the latest toy?'

'Of course they didn't.' Dominy could have been irritated but he knew that this wasn't a silly question. It was an invitation to take the shutters down. 'They're much too professional and much too secure, but we're the Security Executive and I do have certain contacts.' He shrugged again. 'Call it a legitimate guess from the half-truths and hints they gave me. I don't say I'm right but I do say I could be.'

'If the government ordered a thing like that then the government has a death wish.'

'I'm sure they didn't order it—these affairs have a horrible private momentum. You know what scientists are, they crash on in blinkers. However it happened our masters are now stuck with it. Probably the Americans too since that place and Fort Detrick are hand in glove.'

'Oh God,' Laver said.

'God, I'm afraid, may be somewhat in point. Seyer is in with this James or Jacky Dolan. Jacky D he calls himself.'

'That evangelist clown!'

'A lot of people don't think so.'

'And what people.'

'Perhaps. Anyway, Seyer is on what they call the Management Committee. It fixes Jacky's meetings and so on.'

'And you're suggesting that Seyer might spill what he knows to this Jacky D?' Laver corrected himself. 'Or rather spill what he knew a few weeks ago before he broke himself up physically and went wholly to pieces mentally. Before, in fact, they had to retire him.' Richard Laver frowned. 'It wouldn't be quite up-to-date no doubt, but it would certainly be enough to put another scientist on the scent.'

'There's no evidence he's that feeble yet, but I'm entitled to remind you of two things you said yourself: first that he broke up badly, and it's getting much worse and quickly; and secondly you spoke of a developed social conscience. What's certain is that he leans on Jacky.'

'God-walloping evangelism. The last infirmity of noble mind.' Laver spoke with a contempt which he seldom

8

allowed himself but recovered his urbanity at once. 'I'm hoping you're exaggerating.'

'I hope so too but you never know. When a brilliant brain goes to pieces . . .' He let it float.

'I'll admit I've heard of it happening before. Wallis went into a monastery, Edwards tried to geld himself. Seyer might try to buy salvation.'

'You know him—I don't.'

'Not well but it doesn't matter. What matters is the situation. I know nothing of science but I've learnt something of how it works. There's always a point of balance. You research away for months and years, make your experiments, watch your controls. Then suddenly it goes one way or the other, success or failure, black or white. Seyer won't know what's happened in the last few critical weeks since he left, but he'll know everything up to the crisis. Everything.' Laver tapped Charles Russell's desk. 'He could save a rival scientist years.'

'If he talked he would.'

'If he talked or foolishly let it slip. I'm afraid he's pretty foolish. . . . Was there anything else of interest where you went?'

'I can't be sure. Have you ever heard of a Victor Lomax?'

'Never. Who's he?'

'He's on the Management Committee too.'

'So's that frightful Field Marshal. More fool Mr. Lomax.'

'But he isn't a fool, he's an up-and-coming business man. What's he doing in that gallery?'

'Publicity perhaps. Contacts and sales promotion.'

'And if it isn't contacts and sales promotion?'

'Then I wouldn't much like the sound of him.'

2

On his frequent visits to London Paul Frei took two rooms at Brown's Hotel, though he never called them a suite nor even thought of them as such. He would have considered that pretentious and he detested all pretensions. Nor had he need of the symbols of status, only of somewhere to talk with convenience. Enormously rich and powerful men could afford to ignore the Rolls-Royce and the travelling secretary, and Frei was authentically rich and powerful. He had interests in German steel, Italian shipping, a useful share in a chain of hotels covering most of Europe west of the Curtain. Above all he bossed Continental, controlling it directly, and Continental could compete with the giants, with Monsanto and even with I.C.I.

He was talking now to a severely dressed Englishman with the air of an accountant or solicitor. He was still in fact the latter, a partner in a small but respectable City firm, which gave him almost perfect cover for his second and much more lucrative profession. He would have been sincerely horrified if you had called him a criminal, and indeed he had never thought of a crime in the sense that he had originated one. What he did was provide the services, the contacts, the organization. The last especially, for he had a talent for the practical which had been frustrated in the law. His reputation was now in the highest class, so high that a man like von Frei was employing him. Frei was saying now in his tycoon's voice:

'So you follow the position?'

'Perfectly, Baron.'

Paul von Frei frowned. He never used the 'von' in his name, and the country which now protected him (it had cost him a great deal of money) didn't recognize his title. In any case he wished ardently to forget it. Being a Junker baron was bad for business.

'I have made my own arrangements for obtaining the information I require.' Frei's English was perfect but sometimes stilted. 'I own this man Victor Lomax, a director of Farrell and Haye.'

'Which you could buy without noticing it if the prospects seemed worth while to you.'

'No doubt, but they do not. But the firm does have a connection with that Establishment. They specialize in bio-chemicals, so the Establishment gives them some donkey work, the sort which your Mandarin scientist is often too grand to handle himself. That's how I got my line to Victor Lomax.'

The severely dressed Englishman straightened his tie. It was a dark blue tie with stripes which were barely separated, and he wore it rather too much for contemporary taste. Frei thought of him privately as simply Striped Tie. 'So Victor Lomax,' Tie said, 'whom you've now suborned—'

'It wasn't very difficult.'

Frei was thinking it had been easy. . . . The typical English second-rater. He dressed very smartly but quite without elegance. Frei's vocabulary was extensive and he'd found the right word at once. Victor Lomax was dapper, and venal too. Not that Frei blamed him. He wasn't a man to indulge moral judgements, and he knew about Farrell and Haye as well. These English family firms! Victor Lomax was competent, he'd doubled their sales, but a seat on the board was as far as he'd go for he wasn't a Farrell or even a Haye, he hadn't a pound of the equity—never would have. Naturally he'd taken the orthodox steps: Paul Frei knew that too since he never considered corruption without unqualified information about his prospect. There'd been a certain Miss

Farrell, Miss Prudence Farrell, not quite young now and not so pretty. Lomax had pursued her and she'd finally turned him down.

Now Lomax was frustrated and bitter, an almost perfect target for the attentions of Paul von Frei. He was a pretty good salesman but not outstanding, he couldn't walk out to another firm and be utterly sure they'd snap him up. So ask for more money? He'd probably done it often and maybe got it. But after ten thousand, say, who wanted income? Lomax would be a great attender of business lunches and Frei could hear him saying it to a neighbour: 'Of course I don't mind paying my surtax. For useful things, that is. Like nuclear weapons and an efficient Immigration Service, but when it comes to paying for coloured layabouts I stick.'

Von Frei didn't like Victor Lomax much, he was suspect of being a fascist fool, which was something he'd never been himself. An aristocrat, he'd detested Hitler and once had barely escaped with his life. Striped Tie knew the story or he wouldn't have accepted von Frei's commission. So Paul Frei was no fascist and that was good, but he was now a tycoon, a self-made one at that, a formidable, rich and dangerous man. Which made him an excellent customer.

'You have hopes of this Lomax?' Striped Tie was asking.

'Hopes worth a hundred thousand tax free if and when he delivers. Moreover he has started well. Getting on to that Management Committee was intelligent.' For the first time Frei smiled. 'He must have suffered intolerably, prayed and sung, gone through the whole damned hoop. Then they'd have given a Counsellor and he'd be expected to confess his sins. I've heard of a man who picked the wrong one. The Counsellor tried to seduce him.'

Striped Tie smiled politely, though privately he was rather shocked. With the tie he was wearing he shouldn't have been, or perhaps he'd seen too much of it young. 'There's something I don't follow,' he said.

'You must tell me what.'

'What you want is in Mervin Seyer's head and Mervin Seyer has broken up. Since he's eating out of this Jacky D's hand why don't you just proposition Jacky? That strikes me as more direct than employing Lomax.'

'I will ask you another question as answer. What motive has Jacky D to serve me? Money? He has enough for his modest needs and the prospect of more.'

Striped Tie nodded briefly. That might be right or it might be wrong but it was disciplined thinking, he couldn't refute it. In any case Frei had decided already and he wasn't a man you argued with. Striped Tie took his time to think, then said:

'If you've got your own line through Lomax how can my organization help?'

'I told you I had fair hopes of Lomax, good enough at any rate to give him a clear first run at Seyer. But Seyer, as you said yourself, is eating out of Dolan's hand, and for the reason I have just given you I've no connection with Dolan at all. So suppose Seyer talked to Dolan first, there's no knowing what Dolan would do with the story.'

'But why should Seyer talk to Dolan?'

'You said he was eating out of his hand.'

'But I didn't say he was ga-ga yet.'

Frei said patiently: 'You don't know scientists as I do. They're peculiar, especially peculiar when they suddenly get religion as Seyer has. It is odd how the basest forms attract them. You have heard about that spiritualist? He thought he was talking to a Red Indian control of his; he thought the medium was in a trance. But he wasn't talking to a Red Indian, the medium wasn't in trance at all. She was an experienced agent. And on the other side of the fence, the respectable side, I suspect there are parish priests with secrets

DD—B

from the confessional which would start a war tomorrow. Thank God they are trained and experienced men. This Jacky D is not.'

'I follow the danger but I don't see what I can do. Are you suggesting Jacky D disappear?'

'By no means—that would be fatal. I don't doubt you could arrange it, but if Jacky D, er, disappeared, the whole circus would disappear with him, Committee and all. And with it Lomax's contact with Seyer.'

'Quite correct, but where does it take us? So long as Seyer remains in the state he is, the wreck of a fine brain with something inside which you're anxious to know, so long as Jacky's the man he is—'

'But what man is he? At the moment he's riding the crest of a wave, and if Seyer gave him something he shouldn't Jacky might choose to use it. That is our danger. He's got a platform and an audience. It would really be very tempting to spring a sensation.'

'Very.'

'But if Jacky were discredited, who would listen and who believe? Perhaps his hard core but he'd lose the rest. Really discredited, disastrously discredited.'

'How?'

Paul von Frei told him.

When Striped Tie had gone Frei lit a cigar. There was something he hadn't told Striped Tie though he believed in briefing his agents thoroughly. But it was a contingency, not worth mentioning yet. A discredited Jacky *would* have motive, a broken career-less man would want money and fast. And that could be a second string if Frei ever had need to use it.

It hadn't been curiosity which had brought Richard Laver to the Rally for Christ that evening: the words alone made him squirm in a sweaty embarrassment. It had been an unflinching sense of duty. There could be nothing at this Rally which he couldn't equally well learn by discreet inquiry, even by despatching a subordinate as his eyes and ears. Nothing, but in another sense everything, for when Russell had been pressed for a parting word of wisdom he'd said simply that time spent on recce was seldom wasted. It was a cliché—no doubt, but that didn't make it silly. An eminent scientist, lately of a highly secret Establishment, had gone over the edge of what any normal scientist would consider basic sanity; the Establishment was one which Laver deplored and feared, or at least he deplored the world which made it necessary, and it was now on the verge of some shattering new horror, perhaps had even reached it; the eminent scientist, now galloping into senility, had found religion in its crudest and least attractive form, a blister-raising evangelist with a Bible groggy from punching it. It was a frightening situation, potentially dangerous. This deplorable evangelist was well worth a personal look-see. That, Laver knew, would produce no new facts, but at least he'd get the smell of him.

He was sitting now taking his bearings. He had never in his life been to a revivalist meeting but had seen snatches in newsfilms and a short programme on TV. But that had been rather different, the major league: a backing choir of hundreds, all in white, the hall in West London with a crowd like a Cup Final, the calculated darknesses, then the spotlight on that brassily handsome face, all the techniques of an American college football game. This wasn't in that class at all. There was a choir, it was true, but thirty at most, and they were belting a hymn out smartly:

> *Pull for the shore, sailor,*
> *Pull for the shore,*
> *Tum-tum the rolling billow,*
> *TUM all the more.*

It sounded like that but Laver wasn't quite sure. It wasn't in Ancient and Modern or even the English Hymnal.

He was conscious of a man with a collection box, in fact an open bucket. Richard Laver considered that shrewd—you could see what your neighbour put in it. No discreet leather bags in the delicate Anglican manner. He put in a pound but it wasn't blackmail. It was what he gave on Sundays. He still went to church on Sundays, or he did when it was too cold for golf, too early for lunch or a rubber of bridge, but he went without faith, with a certain nostalgia, a gesture to days which would never return. He couldn't accept a word of it but thought no less of a man who did.

No indeed, and why should he? But this was distressingly different from the mind pragmatism of the established church. Laver looked at the platform. There was a microphone at the front of it and, at the back, on uncomfortable chairs, a row of men and women who sat rigidly, not at ease. Laver began to place them, speculating. First there was Mervin Seyer, about whom he needn't speculate. He looked extraordinarily frail and there was a stick between his knees. It was hot up there under the pitiless arcs, and when a swinging fan caught it his fine white shock floated up in a sort of halo. He looked extremely impressive and slightly insane. Next to him was a Negro, though he was far from the type which the word suggested. He wasn't much darker than *café au lait* with a fine straight nose and hooded eyelids. Laver wondered about the Negro but a glance round the hall explained his presence. One man in three had his racial roots in Africa. Richard Laver nodded quietly for he liked to see things fit. Jacky Dolan, alias Jacky D, had been a missionary in Africa, where he'd cut his evangelist teeth on the African race. And very good at it they said he'd been. He had just the touch of simple passion, real or assumed, Laver couldn't tell.

And now he was aiming higher, very much higher. That Field Marshal, for instance: he was looking very lean and fit. Every one knew he was mad as a hare, but he'd been the *général de matériel* once who had had all the breaks and had used them admirably. Laver's eye moved down the line again. . . . Three professional do-gooders whom he could place at once—a man, two women—the sort which nipped on to any bandwagon if they thought it was going their way. Then the progressive bishop whom Laver loathed. He *would* be there, he'd *have* to be there. After all it was advertisement and he had to keep in the public eye. If he wasn't in the limelight he was nothing and he knew it. Beside him two men whom Laver could easily place again. They were gentlemen from the country, obstinately discharging what they conceived to be their duty. Laver knew this type too and didn't despise it for he had seen it in war and he knew its virtues. They weren't very bright, they could bore you rigid; they could lose a patrol on some stupid mistake, but they never lied or let you down and they died with their handmade boots on.

At the end of the line was a man who didn't fit. He was younger for one thing and better dressed, too dressy for normal tastes by half. Not quite flashy but somehow wrong. Damn it, the man was a dapper. He looked as alien as an actress at a country vicarage garden fête, and Laver could sense he was cruelly bored, though he was hiding the fact with a sort of grim discipline. He was interesting—very.

The hymn finished on words which Laver missed and the bishop advanced to the microphone. He wasn't clothed as his rank ordained he should dress and Laver preferred that a prince of his church should dress as his office required of him. But his skill wasn't questionable. He was the fill-in man and he filled in splendidly, warming the audience gently but not too much, not stealing the big man's thunder. It was all about fellowship, the fellowship of their Common Master. The capitals came over with practised ease. Many in the hall tonight would have different doctrines from those he held. (What were they? Laver wondered, for no man knew. There was that book of his but it hadn't been intelligible. A passage or two, but those had been heretical. A few centuries ago and the Dominicans would have burnt him.) So any differences didn't matter in the fellowship of the Living Christ. A Common Master then, a common goal. A common ideal—the word wasn't too strong. All welcome tonight to a man who had picked up the torch and dared to bear it.

There was a round of applause and His Lordship sat down. Two women advanced on the microphone and Laver shrank. They began to sing off-key in what in his youth had been called close harmony. This meant that one was on note, the other just off it. Laver, a lover of opera, groaned aloud. They sang with lugubrious gusto:

> Glorious Jesus, Lovely Jee,
> Come to my heart and comfort me.

Had he really heard that? He couldn't believe it. He could have used that bucket and not to put money in.

The pain ended at last and the lights went out dramatically. A single spot shone on the microphone now and Laver began to count slowly. At the tenth count precisely Jacky D was in the spotlight.

A sort of gasp went round the smallish hall, a tightening of the senses, a sensible shiver. He was pulling back the sheets on a well-loved bed, he was going to give them value. Ah . . .

Laver listened, trying not to. Jacky was brilliant, Jacky was intolerable. He didn't mind what he said, what nerve he plucked. Perhaps this was genius, this utter disregard for any normal reserve or decency. The Blood of the Lamb, the

Nails of the Cross. And what was he saying, this terrible thing? Laver looked at his watch: thirty minutes had gone and he didn't believe it. Thirty minutes of Jacky—eternal salvation. Not a word about God's Grace. Stand up and be counted. Come forward and take my hand. Here and now. I ask you to do it the hard way.

The hard way, hell. The hard way was prayer and fasting, a wrestling with the angel, death. Death, then an unimagined life. That is if the finger fell on you.

. . . Oh God, oh God.

The front two rows stood up and blocked the gangways. The houselights came on and for a moment nothing happened. It was certain this wasn't usual. Ordinarily men and women would start to move, in ones and twos towards the platform and the hungrily waiting Counsellors, an increasing flood. But now they were cut off and the risen sat down. The front two rows began to chant rhythmically:

'Jacky D is an impostor. Out, out, out.'

There was silence in the hall, then a mutter of anger. Laver looked at the front two rows with care. They seemed perfectly ordinary citizens. The men had their hair short, the women wore skirts; these weren't professional protesters. But clearly they knew their business.

'To hell with Jacky. *Out.*'

The mutter from the hall began to rise. Richard Laver didn't like it. One man in three was of other race, and though Laver had nothing against it he knew it well. It was quick to anger, as quick to violence.

Jacky D stood uncertain, raising his arms. The gesture was symbolic perhaps, but it was totally ineffective.

'Go back to your black men. Go, go, go.'

The mutter was now an angry swell and Richard Laver looked over his shoulder. There was an exit only three rows behind and he noted its presence gratefully.

On the platform Jacky was silent.

It happened quite smoothly, on a signal from some leader he couldn't see. They began to throw deliberately, almost in volleys, the soft stuff from pockets and innocent handbags on laps, eggs and tomatoes, rubbish.

Jacky Dolan took cover, doubling up behind the lectern. There was a sudden shocked silence, then the Field Marshal's parade-ground roar, destructively clear.

'Get up, man. Stand *up*.'

With an infinite caution Jacky D straightened up and the first and the last brick caught him. It caught him high on the chest and it couldn't have hurt him seriously but it finished him for the evening. He grabbed at the lectern and his hand fell on the microphone. His cry of pure terror, inhumanly magnified, came out as the yell of a frightened giant. His face in the spotlight had always been white, now it was twisted with shameless fear. Holding the microphone still he gasped, and the relays picked it up as a broken sob. Every man and woman present heard it and they saw. One moment Jacky D was there, the next he wasn't.

The hall was in an uproar now, men seething towards the platform, shouting. For a second Richard Laver was left in doubt, owning no taste for rough houses, far less to be trampled in what looked serious. Discretion urged him to leave while he could but his appetite for experience won. He stood up to see better.

The Field Marshal was on his feet again and somehow he reached the microphone.

'Ladies and gentlemen—'

'*Siddahn.*'

'Friends, fellow Christians—'

'Silly old bastard.' (Perfectly true.) 'Murderer. Assassin.' (A little unfair.)

The Field Marshal retired. He'd always been rather good

at it.

From the row of uncomfortable platform chairs a second man rose lithely. Laver saw it was the Negro. He walked deliberately to the lectern, picking the mike from its tangled flex, putting it close to his mouth but not too close. He didn't speak but began to sing. The sheer surprise of it made them hesitate. The banal but splendid words rolled out, part of the poor patrimony of every man present.

> *Oh God our help in ages past,*
> *Our hope for years to come.*

The powerful untutored bass boomed on, untaught but entirely pure and true. He was singing as nature had told him to sing, with passion but also a real control. One or two voices joined him, then more and more. The organ came in but was drowned ignominiously.

Richard Laver recovered his hat and coat. He could see that the police had arrived in some strength but the police would hardly be needed now. The disturbers had slipped away and the rest . . .

They were singing uninhibitedly now, the hall was a roar of defiant sound. Defying what? Richard Laver wondered. The Prince of Darkness? Unlikely. For very few believed in him, even the absent Jacky played that one cool. The appalling world they lived in? Yes, perhaps. Their own shame at violence escaped by a whisker? Perhaps again, and again perhaps not.

He found a cab and went home in it thoughtfully.

3

Margaret Seyer was lunching with Peter Dinoba. She was civilized about coloured skins, neither secretly defensive because a man's pigment wasn't her own nor defiantly committed to the doctrine there were no differences. In any case it wasn't easy to think of Peter Dinoba as a Negro. He wasn't much darker than a European who'd been sunbathing, and the cut of his features was if anything semitic. He had a firm full mouth but the lips weren't fleshy, the whites of his eyes were entirely clear. The folklore of his race had an ancient tradition: they had come down to west Africa in centuries long forgotten, migrating from the middle Nile, and those whose business was to know such things were inclined to believe the tale had basis. It was Margaret Seyer's unspoken hunch that he didn't think of himself as a Negro at all. That was a guess but there was evidence to back it. His country had a coastal belt and she knew he disliked its inhabitants. He had never said this and never would but she'd also have bet he despised them. He'd think of them as black men, a sort of monkey. Secretly, of course—he'd never admit it. Nor would he even consider the words since he wouldn't betray the country he loved passionately. It was free now and he was proud of it.

Margaret watched him deal with the waiter. He was doing it very well, she thought, quite sure of himself but not overbearing; he wasn't expecting insolence from a waiter and wouldn't receive it; he had the ease of assured position but none of its arrogance, even unconsciously. And he was really extremely handsome. Margaret had a mezzotint of Peter Dinoba in her home, or rather it was an ancestor, a Georgian blood in the heyday of the Bath Pump Room. He had the same hooded eyes, the full and sensual but well-cut mouth. Take his absurd half-wig away, paint him the colour of well-kept parquet, and there would be Peter Dinoba, living. He would have something of the character too, the air of inherited ease, the patina hiding an unquestioned masculinity.

It had occurred to Margaret Seyer that she might have to be careful with Peter Dinoba. She was too experienced to suppose that an attachment to an African wouldn't have complications, and her life at the moment was sufficiently complicated. Her father, for instance—his mind was fading fast. Well, she could handle that and would: what wasn't in the contract was the fact that he'd got religion. She had nothing against it, it could often smooth old age and make it serene, but her father's chosen brand of it was simply making him miserable. There was nothing in this of peace, only of fear. Conscience—saving his soul. He had much on his conscience to answer for and she knew enough of his work to guess at what, but if he had to make his peace with God she'd have preferred a God she could recognize and respect, one you could talk to directly or one of his priests. Experienced, trained, all-knowing in God's name, discreet—they'd let you off the hook since they had the power. Jacky D was just a platform star and his private beliefs she didn't know, but Jacky held her father in the hollow of his reluctant hand. She would concede the reluctance for certainly it was evident. Jacky D fished souls in gross and raw, not the delicate waters of individual conscience, but Mervin Seyer depended on him like an ageing dog on a well-loved master. That was irony but a very poor joke. Margaret Seyer found it frightening.

She said warmly: 'You were splendid last night. You saved the whole thing.' She hesitated on the next sentence for she knew that Jacky D held Dinoba too. The dreadful man *had* something. It was inexplicable but it was there, this appalling power to excite and then to hold. Her father was one thing, for a psychologist could no doubt explain the infatuation of an old scientist in terms at least acceptable to another of his profession. Her father, then, was one thing but Peter Dinoba quite another. He wasn't an ageing scientist who had smashed himself up in a car and never recovered; he was an acutely intelligent African in the plenitude of his powers. So she hesitated but added it.

'You didn't run away.' She put on the pronoun a delicate but inviting emphasis.

Peter Dinoba ducked it. 'Of course I didn't—how could I run? There were two or three hundred there—my own people.'

Margaret Seyer sighed softly. What she wanted to know was Jacky D's future—had that evening's fiasco finished him? She fervently hoped it had but couldn't say so. She began to fish discreetly.

'Of course you've seen the newspapers?'

'Yes,' he said grimly, 'I've seen the newspapers.'

So had Margaret Seyer. *The Times* had merely reported it, the *Telegraph* been ironic in the column it hoped was irony. But the *Guardian* had gone further. In one of its thoughtful leaders it had speculated pontifically. . . . Was there possibly some connection between the current wave of drug-taking and these extraordinary outbursts of mass hysteria? The word wasn't too strong. No open-minded man (the implication was inescapable that all its readers were open-minded) would object to an honest revivalism. It might have aspects which were distasteful to the cultured readers of the *Guardian* but no doubt there were lesser men who could take good from it. The leader didn't say this in terms but contrived to convey it perfectly. But mass hysteria was something else, not distasteful but simply frightening. A man who peddled it on purpose was very dangerous, anti-social.

These had been the heavies in the varied but quite predictable veins, but the tabloids had joyfully pounced on it. Margaret's own favourite had put it squarely on the front page, a cruelly revealing picture, Jacky's white face contorted with terror. And the simple caption had done the rest.

GOD-MAN LEGS IT

Would it finish him, Margaret wondered, and if so when? She had to know. She'd been meeting some curious people since her father joined the Committee, and Peter Dinoba was the only one she trusted. Ask the Field Marshal? He'd waffle for an hour and tell her nothing. That bishop? He'd brush her off. Victor Lomax? She didn't like him. It had to be Peter Dinoba and she'd have to handle him carefully. The least hint what she was after and he'd drop her like a red hot stone.

She wouldn't like that.

'What's going to happen?' She asked it non-committally.

'It all depends on Thursday evening. We've been lucky, I suppose. Jacky's been trying to make telly for months and they wouldn't even consider it. Now he's news, of a sort, and they ask him at once.'

'A programme of his own?' She was horrified but hid it.

'Not exactly a programme but he's on somebody else's. You know the sort of thing. Seven-minute interviews and the guest does the talking.' He smiled. 'Jacky can talk fast, you know.'

'He can indeed.'

'If he brings it off it could restore the whole position.'

He was loyal, she thought, and she liked them loyal. He'd been missionary-educated, baptized as a Christian, and coming on to Oxford he'd lost his faith. He hadn't been happy, had flirted with the other religion, communism. And then one evening he'd gone to a Rally of Jacky's. . . . Wham! All in an evening, just like that, the Dolan spiritual sucker punch. She deplored it but had to accept the fact.

So almost at once he'd joined the Committee, where indubitably he'd been useful. Useful and loyal and still intelligent. Not all the Committee were that or anything like it. Her father was on for his name and fame, and in his moments of rare lucidity Mervin Seyer was still impressive. Alas that she couldn't foretell them. The Field Marshal was mildly crazy, the bishop sought only publicity—good publicity. Already he'd started to cool from Jacky. Three others were cranks, two honest but very stupid. That left only Victor Lomax. . . .

Victor Lomax was somehow suspect. She couldn't say why but was perfectly sure of it. She rather thought her father thought so too. So it had to be Peter, she had to accept her risks. She asked him deliberately:

'If he makes a good impression—'

'He could surely make a come-back. Yes.'

She said: 'I hope he does.'

It was a lie.

Paul Frei had in fact been over-insuring. Jacky had had no intention of airing the affairs of a secret Establishment on the platforms of evangelist Rallies. Not that he didn't realize that something critical was afoot: that old fool Seyer had told him so, miserably, racked by conscience, seeking the sort of spiritual balm which Jacky didn't believe in and didn't dispense. There'd been nothing in this alone for that much was out. Many journalists suspected it, though it was no sort of story without the facts, Wiltshire was plagued on fine week-ends by not-so-young men with banners, women in jeans which no longer quite fitted them, a rabble tolerated by its elders for its total ineffectiveness, despised by the really young for the same good reason. Besides, that was politics, and Jacky had learnt in Africa that to survive in his profession at all he must keep very clear of politics.

He'd been a missionary, a sincere one till his marriage had

almost broken him. Doris Dolan—he hated her. She'd been a missionary too and she'd determined to marry him. He hadn't fancied her in his bed or out, but she'd been to their Supervisor and shamelessly nobbled him. . . . So in a country so full of temptations would it not be wiser . . . ? It was better to marry than burn in hell, and the help of a good woman, one dedicated to the same fine end . . .

He had asked for a transfer but his Supervisor had refused it and the Coast was too hot for a struggle he saw no end to. So he'd married her and bedded her and his life had become a nightmare. Now he hated her without reserve. She was always right; she *had* to be right. Her ideas hadn't changed since she'd left that horrible school of hers, and now she taught the same ideas unenlightened by any spark of grace. She was bossy, Spartan and dedicated—a terror. Those shattering basilisk phrases 'I must say' and 'To tell the truth'. She always told the truth, God damn her. Not like Anna Vescovi who was really a shocking liar. Anna was tolerant, amorous, easily gay; not the classical evangelical virtues. Spaghetti halfway up the walls, minestrone in the wash-basin. But Anna belonged to a later age, a bonus to the original stroke of luck.

He had just about been desperate when it had come to him out of the blue. The head of his organization had been visiting his station, coming to one of Jacky's meetings. Jacky hadn't seen him there but he remembered the evening per-fectly. He'd been in black despair and he hadn't cared, not what he said nor how he said it. He'd felt contempt for him-self and contempt for his God and he'd taken it out on his sweating audience. He'd pulled all the stops out, he'd let them have it boiling and strong, without reserve, indecently.

The results had quite astonished him, a hundred conver-sions and maybe more. Conversions were very important to the Mission he happened to work for. It was hard-gutted and

Scottish and counted heads relentlessly.

After the meeting the Chief had come up, making a proposition which had changed Jacky's life entirely. Mr. Dolan, the Chief had earnestly said, had certainly been blessed with Special Gifts. Jacky remembered the phrase with a tolerant smile. And it wasn't God's Will that Special Gifts should be Wasted. Not that the African Brother was Waste, but there were Richer Pastures, a Wider Field. To cut the rigmarole short he had offered a year, twelve months in England at the Mission's expense. The offer had staggered Jacky D but the Chief hadn't quite finished. He was a mean-souled creature and couldn't resist it, the barb which would stick and torment for months; he simply wasn't capable of a gift given gracefully. Instead he said with his Judas smile:

'In England certain, er, defects of character will not matter so much as here.'

Jacky had known what he meant: he'd meant that girl. Not that it had been serious. Now he wished it had been.

Jacky had never forgiven him, even now that some success had come. For that had been more than a year ago, he was out of his contract with his original employers. He had his own Committe now, and they made his arrangements and paid him a fair salary. But he wanted much more than that and he meant to get it, the choirs of hundreds, the people who really mattered, the solid fame. Partly his need was money, money to buy off Doris, to pre-empt Anna, but there was more to it than money. He wanted success, the real big time. He had lost his faith by now but he hardly missed it; instead he had his power. He knew its limitations too but within them he was king of it. Sometimes it almost frightened him. His public was soft as rotten cheese, drug addicts in their different way, but also they were his instrument and he knew perfectly how to play on it.

He too was hooked though he didn't know it, hooked in

the rat race of the not quite first class Bible-puncher's league.

Success, he thought—it hadn't been far away then he'd cravenly chucked it. He too had seen the newspapers and they'd made him writhe. But these same contemptuous newspapers had put him on to telly. The invitation from Wood Lane had been a life-raft to a drowning man but he hadn't at first seen quite how to use it. An interview too, so they wouldn't let him rant and rave. He used the words to himself without shadow of shame. What he needed was something to pin them quickly, something to make them switch off and discuss him.

It had come to him unexpectedly for it had been flatly against his previous plans. It would have to be political and he knew exactly what would serve his end.

. . . That old donkey Mervin Seyer. Jacky wasn't a wicked man, far less merely malicious, and he had a genuine human sympathy for what was now the wreck of a once fine brain. It was just that the man was a bore, a drag. Jacky's art was to pluck men's consciences, twisting them, tearing and torturing, but give him an individual one and he didn't know what to do with it. So poor old Seyer—he'd gone over the hill. A car smash and quick senility, on top of it an abrasive conscience. The latter was quite explicable for Jacky knew Seyer's work and was thankful he didn't do it. But the man *had* done it, for prestige or money, God alone knew, and now, in decline, he was trying to shrive himself. Let him go to a priest then, that wasn't Jacky's trade. But Seyer kept coming back to him, a dog to unhappy vomit. Several times Jacky had shut him up, for he had a healthy respect for official secrets. As an evangelist he wanted none of them and as a citizen he was scared.

So Jacky had shut the old man up but not always quite completely. Plenty of people already suspected that the Establishment was working on some fresh horror, and most of them also suspected that it was some new and really appalling germ. What none of them knew was the new germ's nature. Jacky D did for he wasn't stupid. The old man had been mooning away one night and Jacky had hardly been listening, thinking of Anna Vescovi, of the forthcoming Rally at Bournemouth. Bournemouth had sounded promising, he'd wow them in Bournemouth. Yes . . .

. . . What was that he had heard though he hadn't wished to? Selective Pigmentation Disease. Or S.P.D.

He had silenced Mervin Seyer at once and had tried to forget the words but failed. He remembered them now with gratitude—Selective Pigmentation Disease. It was dynamite. It didn't hit you at once as did phrases with Hell and Death in them, but after a second's hesitation the impact was all the greater. The hearer got the message, yes indeed. Of course it was rather too formal and stiff, you couldn't go on mouthing Selective Pigmentation Disease for long. But nor would you have to. State it once, then use the initials. S.P.D. It had a sort of sibilant menace all its own.

Jacky considered it carefully since it wasn't his established form. It had the bite, it would make them sit up, but the political risks apart, and he'd have to take them, could he *do* it? Could he put it over and make it stick? Another flop would be fatal.

He decided he could—he'd have to. Of course he'd need to change his style, no rhetoric, no banging the lectern. Instead he'd sit at a table quietly, staring straight at the millions of faces.

. . . In the terrible world we lived in there was only one Hope. A terrible world? We knew that well, but did we know how terrible? There were sins unnumbered, affronts to God, but all had been atoned for. Yes, even Selective Pigmentation Disease. Think on that and then come to God's Mercy. S.P.D. . . . Millions of men and women,

30

children too, people selected for death by other men. Wicked men? We were all responsible.

He could do it and do it well. He'd be desperately serious, agonizingly sincere. And he must remember to keep his hands still.

He began to swear softly, not in anger but in quiet relief. It was a habit which had crept up on him and at first he had hardly noticed it, like the loss of his personal faith which had seeped away: the one day he'd been a Christian, the next a man who peddled Christ. Swearing had come to him gently too, perhaps an unconscious surrogate. He still couldn't swear in public but he swore happily in private, deliciously enjoying it. He swore when alone and he sometimes swore at Doris. She only looked him up and down in that flat disapproving way of hers. So now he was swearing quietly, rather well, taking God's name in vain and a great deal more. He'd always known the basic words for he'd never been the priggish type, and Africa had added to his original and native range. There was some mighty fine swearing in African English, colourful obscenities breathing fire and life and simple guts. Jacky D had a vocabulary which a bummaree would have envied.

He finished his bout of release and felt much better, walking to a mirror and looking in it thoughtfully. The solid face looked back at him, sincere and open, Jacky D still, with Special Gifts.

Yes, he could do it, and yes, he would. He'd get right back and he'd do it Thursday.

Paul Frei had been very angry indeed but by now had recovered his normal poise. The matter had struck him as grossly unfair. You laid careful plans and they worked to the letter: Jacky D had been humiliated, people were laughing when not openly malicious, and in any other country he'd be finished for good and all. And what do those strange English do? They put him on television. For months he'd been trying to make it and they wouldn't have hide or hair of him, then he makes a public fool of himself and they hand him seven minutes of priceless time. A preposterous race, entirely unpredictable. One couldn't be blamed if one failed to foresee their vagaries but was entitled to resent it when a total lack of logic endangered carefully considered plans. Seven minutes on telly could be a very long time and Jacky, whatever you thought of him, was an artist in his detestable way. For reasons which had seemed sensible Frei had decided to discredit Jacky D; he'd had a logical, even an elegant plan which had worked very well in practice. Jacky D had looked the clown he was. And now? They'd handed him the chance to climb right back.

The English were extraordinary but Frei was talking again to the Englishman in the striped tie.

'So you understand the new objective?'

'Perfectly, thank you. This man mustn't be allowed to re-establish his position.' The man in the tie lit a Turkish cigarette. 'A pity in a way. Rather a gifted rascal. By the way, the arrangements we made at that Rally were satisfactory?' He permitted himself a half-smile. 'I confess I rather enjoyed their making.'

'I'm glad you get some pleasure from your work.'

The bland legal face went suddenly hard. 'If that was reproof I am not for reproving. Please remember that we need each other.'

'I hadn't forgotten, no.'

'Then what do you want me to do? I'm clear about the end but not the means. As I understand it you want this appearance on telly killed, just as we killed that Rally. The obvious way to achieve that end would be simply to kill this Jacky.'

'You could do it?'

'Of course. You can kill anyone in England given adequate organization and keep a very fair chance that you'll never be touched yourself. Anybody, that is, but just two men."

'Are you going to tell me?'

'Certainly. A Prime Minister, alas, and a simple policeman. Kill either of those and the heat comes on intolerably.' The Englishman tapped his cigarette. 'This Jacky is neither.'

'I told you before why we couldn't kill him.'

'And I've thought of another reason since. If we killed Jacky D we'd bring Security out like a hive of bees. Mervin Seyer was head geneticist at a highly secret Establishment, or he was till he went soft-headed and had to go, only a few weeks ago. In any other country they'd have found some excuse to put him away, but in England they don't do that yet. That's a situation, don't you think? Very troublesome to the authorities—dangerous too. I can't imagine that the Security Executive isn't at least alert to it, though so far it hasn't been active. But leave a body about for the police to play with, a close contact of Mervin Seyer on that Committee, and the Executive would come in at once.'

'I agree,' Frei said, though in fact he hadn't thought like that. No wonder this fixer could command his own price for services. Frei said respectfully: 'You put it very lucidly.'

'In my youth I was trained to be lucid. But I don't quite see what I can do. Short of killing this Dolan—we're agreed we dare not—I don't see how to stop his appearance.'

'But I don't object to his just appearing.'

'No?'

Paul Frei was getting on top again. 'No. And I venture to think you are somewhat oversimplifying.'

'Indeed? How so?'

'We're agreed on a common object at least—this seven

minutes of television mustn't restore Jacky D's prestige. But I doubt if his normal methods could do it. You'll have seen the English papers and so have I. He has slipped too far to get back by banging about and bawling salvation, but the risk remains what it always was, that Seyer may have told him something, even a hint but a hint he could use. I don't mind his going on telly much, what I fear is he'll make a sensation.'

'I'm beginning to see,' the other said.

'Then I'm sure I needn't elaborate but we ought to be straight for the record. If he comes on the box with his usual act I'm prepared to accept the risk of it. I don't think it's a serious one—he won't get back by the usual road. But if he gives even a hint of that Establishment's mysteries, talks about germs or biological warfare . . . In particular I have heard a whisper, a phrase about some disease which selects by colour. So the warning words would be "germ" or "colour", even "select" if the context looked dangerous.'

'I understand now. In effect you want this appearance policed. If he steps across the line, *your* line—'

'You think you could do it?'

'Possibly. I can try.' The Englishman picked his umbrella up. At the door he said with his lawyer's smile: 'We do have an electrician.'

Paul Frei lit a long cigar again. Things were moving his way, he had two chances now. If Lomax succeeded well and good, but a broken James Dolan might also play ball.

4

Laver was talking to Martin Dominy, as much to clear a puzzled mind as in the hope of fresh information. He was groping in the dark still and privately rather edgy, but no man reached Under-Secretary rank without power to conceal he was totally lost, so he asked with an almost normal smile: 'Where have we got to?' He wasn't aware he was using the plural. It had come tripping out quite naturally, as though he'd been sitting for months in Russell's chair.

Dominy was a deliberate man and he considered the question deliberately. 'First take the facts if that's a proper word for them. Russell opens a file and entitles it "S.P.D.—Selective Pigmentation Disease?" The question mark isn't typical. Obviously he got the phrase somewhere, but it must have been in some context he mistrusted since if there'd been any chance of a follow-up he'd have told us where to look for it. But he does send me down to Wiltshire to poke about, and though I've got proof of exactly nothing I'm certain that something's cooking.'

'So far so bad.'

'Then the danger is Mervin Seyer, who knows too much and is insecure. *Vis-à-vis* Jacky Dolan he's especially insecure.'

'What do we know against Jacky Dolan?'

'Nothing. But there's that man on his Committee, Victor Lomax.' Dominy pushed a file across. Lomax wasn't the type to rate a standing dossier at the Executive but in thirty-six hours it had completed a very thorough one.

Richard Laver read it carefully. 'I don't think I should like him much but I don't think that's important either. So here's Victor Lomax on that Committee. Why? He's a director of Farrell and Haye who do antibiotics. You think Farrell and Haye are behind all this?'

'I can't say they're not but I'd lay heavily against it. They're a respectable old family firm. Even if they were otherwise they're not big enough to organize riots at Jacky's Rallies. No, I don't think they're relevant, only their man Lomax.'

'So he isn't on that Committee for Farrell and Haye, and he's hardly likely to be working for himself. Who stands behind him?'

'This isn't a matter of states, I'm sure of that. I rather wish it were. We've a certain experience in dealing with states, our two principal enemies and one very old friend who's not always so friendly. No, I'd guess it was commercial.'

Richard Laver reflected. 'Hell, I hate that. But I've got to admit it could be. Who's in that league?'

'Continental for one—they're big enough.'

'Continental is our old friend Frei—I've read him up already. We've had him on our plate before and he's big enough and wicked enough. To do what, though? How could he use any secret from that Establishment?'

'Perhaps to sell to a government, though again I'd lay odds against it. That isn't Paul Frei's normal form, he prefers his own hands on the levers of power. But if he could get it and study it, find an antidote perhaps . . . Manufacture the stuff and store it . . . And then when the balloon went up he'd have a nation, even a race at ransom. I don't think money interests Frei much. Not any more. He plays for power. If this new thing is really selective by colour of skin and he held an antidote—'

'He'd be rather more powerful than all the world's praesidia.' Laver rose unexpectedly. 'My own car's being serviced and I don't want to take an official one where I'm going. Would you trust me with yours?'

'Of course.'

And now, after two hours motoring, Laver was getting

the feel of the red Alfa; after eighty miles driving he had just about made the change of philosophy. That was the word, he decided at once. His own R-type Bentley was fifteen years old, had had several resprays and the clock showed a hundred thousand. Just about run in. The massive old engine would take anything you gave it, and if a gallon of petrol barely carried you round the corner that was the price of what Laver considered comfort. Rather different in ethos from this delicate but efficient toy. It had the high-revving race-bred engine beloved of the Italian heart, it was fairly quiet inside but noisy out, and in anything like a wind you lost the front. But it would leave the old Bentley standing if you chose to risk your life in it, and Richard Laver, driving it well by now, turned the bright red car through the single-barred gate.

He had come down to Wiltshire as he had gone to Jacky's Rally, not for information but to get the flavour of the place, its aura. A signboard greeted him in the Mandarin manner: PERMISSION TO PROCEED ON THIS ROAD MAY BE ASSUMED WHEN THE GATE IS OPEN BUT THE PUBLIC MUST KEEP TO THE ROAD, and on the wire-mesh fences which fringed it other notices said: DANGER, KEEP OUT. But behind the high fences black and white cows were grazing peacefully. It was all very English. This was still in theory a public road though it could be closed very quickly and sometimes was, and it wasn't the English habit to draw attention to what you might wish to hide. In the States there would have been a peripheral road inside the wire, armed men patrolling it, and watch-towers like a Nazi camp. Here what was sought and partly achieved was an air of the almost casual. These once fine downs were dotted with other establishments, radar and aircraft, only moderately secret. This sinister place sought the impression it was another.

As Laver drove on he was certain that it wasn't. Nobody

challenged him, but he knew that if he left his car, showed symptoms of curiosity, he'd be stopped at once. But he had no intention of testing local security: for one thing it wasn't his business to do so and for another he lacked the technical skill to pry with any profit. The most critical experiment conducted under his nose would tell him nothing, and as for papers he shouldn't see, either they'd be meaningless to a man who wasn't a scientist or they'd be telling him something he knew already, for instance Mervin Seyer's recent movements. A week before he had smashed himself up he'd been in the States at a place called Fort Detrick and he wouldn't have gone to Maryland for amusement. Fort Detrick and this Establishment were on a great deal closer than friendly terms. A government had blindly allowed the liaison and now was lumbered with its bastard. If what Martin Dominy believed were true it could find itself in extreme embarrassment; if what he believed were both true and leaked it could find itself fighting for political survival.

Laver turned right, driving on half a mile, stopping before the administrative building, low, long and white and not ungracious. Another notice board made him smile again: *Chemical Defence Experimental Establishment*. The 'Defence', he decided, was perfectly contemporary, like Ministry of Defence for what was really your War Department. It was perfectly contemporary and also a little shaming, but Richard Laver hadn't motored here to make reflections on the social climate, nor was he greatly interested in the C.D.E.E. He shared Dominy's guess that that side of the Establishment was probably nicely balanced, a balance of terror like another better publicized. *Tabun*, *Sarin* and *Soman*—they were really rather old hat by now. Now you could break down the substance resetting the nerves, *Acetylcholinesterase* or some such gibberish. The unpronounceable mouthful concealed the horror. So GE and GT, VE and VX.

It hardly mattered what you called them since their use was restrained by a single fact, and a man wicked enough to use them, or facing defeat, would know it. If you threw these things round a cringing world the world would throw them back at you. Your own particular horror might be marginally more horrible but it could hardly be a margin to swing the balance. Cold comfort on winter nights for the old, hardly a comfort at all to the ardent young. But it had worked that way in another field.

Let it pass and pray stoutly—there wasn't the same faint hope up this second road. *Microbiological Research Establishment*. No euphemism here about Defence. That was probably accidental but accidentally might be significant. There were plenty of killing diseases known and Laver had once recited some. He'd been whistling in the dark and knew it. Suppose they did get something new: that *could* be decisive. But the risks of infection back would still remain.

Or would they? Dominy's information, or to be accurate his experienced guess, had been that they were working on something selective, selective by the colour of a man's skin. Which would explain why an eminent geneticist had been posted with microbiologists. Laver remembered a casual passage in a newspaper. It had been the heaviest of the heavies and it hadn't been in the context of this bland but frightening Wiltshire down, but it had been the sort of information which Laver unconsciously pigeon-holed and now he remembered it grimly. Two eminent Doctors, one of Cambridge, one of London, had jointly won the Nobel Prize in medicine and physiology. They had deciphered the structure of something called *Deoxyribonucleic acid*, 'the messenger of heredity'.

It could be quite unconnected, but Laver shivered in the late June sun. His conscience must be his own, he must never share it: that was one thing Charles Russell had fiercely insisted on. If it came to a killing you must order it unequivocally, be always too proud for mere connivance. For that you would be answerable to your God if he existed, but Charles Russell hadn't expected that his God would be a fool. He'd be a senior administrator, even more potent than Russell himself; He wouldn't hold it against a colleague that he'd simply done his duty. So you took a man's life and left judgement to your Maker. Human lives—one or two and with real regret. But there were areas of the world which would be happier and more prosperous if their inhabitants were ruthlessly halved, countries where citizens of one colour would secretly break a sigh of relief if citizens of another were simply not there. Put a weapon like that in the hands of some desperate man . . .

Genocide wouldn't be something for understanding and quiet forgiveness. No.

Laver began to drive again, out by another gate, north-west, under the railway bridge and down into the village. It had once been wholly charming but now, like most others, had been vulgarized remorselessly. But there was still a solid manor, three or four smaller but pleasant houses, and Seyer had taken one of them intending to retire there. How long would he live now, if living was what you called it? Richard Laver didn't know and nor did the doctors: he might go on as he was for some time, sliding into senility fast, finally into madness. His brain had been damaged physically but plenty of men lived on with damaged brains. What worried his doctors was something else: Seyer was eating his heart out, quietly destroying himself. Conscience, a load on his soul. These weren't respectable words for high-class doctors.

Laver didn't intend to call on Seyer. He knew him slightly as a kinsman and had lunched at this handsome burgher's house, but that had been in the depths of winter. Now he wanted to look at Seyer's garden. He had files on all the Committee now, eight new, two old, for Seyer and the bishop had been worth their permanent records, Mervin Seyer for his eminence, His Lordship for something distressingly different. These files had been useful but not the end, for papers gave you the facts but little of the essential man. To get that you looked at his bookshelves first or if you couldn't do that then you looked at his garden.

Laver halted the car fifty yards past the house, then walked up to it unobtrusively. It stood well back from the road, the lawn in front. He stood in the shade of the opposite hedge, staring into the garden . . . Em. No geraniums, no alyssum or aubretia, but then this wasn't suburbia. Equally none of the showy stuff which nurserymen tried to load you with. There were Cape hyacinths in an elegant file, a good deal of musk, now almost over, phlox and lychnis and nemesia. Many old-fashioned roses, beautifully kept. Richard Laver nodded approvingly.

He went back to his car and started for London, taking the road up the winding Bourne valley. The Establishment set his teeth on edge, he did not desire to see it again. As he drove he reflected, thinking of Mervin Seyer, not the eminent geneticist but the man who grew musk and ancient roses. He'd had a first-class brain, his papers proved that, but he'd been a good deal more than just another first-class brain. He'd had the garden of a man of taste, even rather a sensitive one. Who'd fallen for this Jacky D, a second-class evangelist who appealed to the crudest and grossest of men. In anything like his normal health Mervin Seyer would have laughed at him.

It was strange but there'd been precedents. The taller the tree the harder it fell and Seyer, in his profession, had been a high one. Richard Laver grimaced. This ex-eminent geneticist now leaned on Jacky Dolan as the only man who could help him, save his soul. It had happened that way so you had to accept it. It might be more fruitful by far to consider Jacky.

There'd been a file on him too and Laver had been intrigued by it, the home in north London, the muslin curtains and crotons in brass ewers, the grim chapel-going rectitude. Then the mission field and its first bright hopes, the impression of fading zeal and drive. On top of it Doris Dolan—what a terror! Six cool and destructive sentences had brought her to a horrible life, mincing, assured, unforgiving, a bitch. It had been death on death till the one great break, the discovery of this scaring talent. So now Jacky lived by it, banging his Bible, bawling his God like a barker outside the Bearded Lady.

A rogue and a sham? Laver didn't know. He was slow to moral judgement and in any case he sympathized. A rogue perhaps, but very likely without knowing it, and as for shams the word was relative. If Jacky was a sham then that bishop was a worse one. Jacky didn't accept a salary from an established church whose doctrines he mined and sapped; he preached the crudest form of Come-and-be-Saved, but no man could call him heretic. And this woman Anna Vescovi —the file had had her too, complete with photograph. So Jacky was a sinner who preached salvation. There had been others much more celebrated. It would really have been surprising if he hadn't attempted to guard his sanity. Doris Dolan had been unmanning him. Put a white man down on some teeming but lonely tropical coast, take the best of his youth, his hopes, perhaps his faith . . .

Laver wouldn't have agreed that he approved of Jacky D. To approve a man meant judging him which was something which Laver seldom did, but he wasn't without an immediate sympathy. Damn it, he almost liked the man and when you did that, approval was irrelevant.

42

He left the car in the garage where Dominy kept it, then took a taxi in the rain to Provost Road. Mary Laver was tidying their daughter's late tea. He raised his eyebrows, she nodded gloomily. 'She's gone out,' she said.

'Some protest again?'

'No, a man.'

'Beard and guitar? Not very clean?'

'Not at all, he was very clean indeed.'

'That makes a nice change.'

'I'm glad you think so.' She hesitated. 'He was coloured.'

He frowned but not at his wife. All race prejudice was disgraceful but it was even more disgraceful to pretend it was non-existent. What one did was to differentiate. He said casually:

'A West Indian?'

'No, she dislikes them. He's a Nigerian, a Hausa, I think, and he was very well dressed in an old-fashioned way. His manners with me were perfectly beautiful. He arrived in a taxi and kept it waiting.' She laughed, not quite easily, but not to hide terror. 'Patty calls him her Black Knight Square.'

'Just so long as it isn't an Indian.'

This time she snorted. 'Patty's a little wild perhaps, but she isn't a perfect bloody fool.'

He turned on the telly fretfully, for he seldom bothered to look at it unless there was something he'd marked in his newspaper, but now he had an empty hour and was ready for once to waste it. It was a programme called simply *People*, interviews with persons in the news. At the moment there was a very fat woman, uncertain of age and of minimal charms. She had invented something but it wasn't clear what. Someone had poached her patent, or so she said, and as she started to name a name they cut her slickly.

Richard Laver sipped his tea and watched on . . . 'And now a man whom many of you will know. Mr. James

Dolan, better known to thousands as Jacky D. Perhaps a controversial figure, and after an incident at one of his Rallies last week . . .'

The smooth tell-nothing voice flowed on but the picture came up behind it, Jacky D but a new one. He was sitting quietly at a table staring straight at the millions of faces. He was enormously solemn, genuinely impressive, and his hands on the table before him were perfectly still.

The lead-in, the harmless question.

' . . . In the terrible world we lived in there was only one Hope. A terrible world? We knew that well but did we know how terrible? There were sins unnumbered, affronts to God, but all had been atoned for. Yes, even Selective—'

He was suddenly on his feet, then collapsed across the table. He pulled himself upright and stood trembling uncontrollably.

The interviewer hesitated. His instinct was to signal for Cut but he didn't entirely trust it. A month ago a visitor had gone into a miming act and the interviewer had cut him cold. He had got into trouble for doing so. There'd been a shoal of letters, protests presenting the dread word censorship. The interviewer had been matted and now he was uncertain. This could be just another act. Evangelists, Bible-punchers . . .

It was not. Jacky was standing there white and shaking, but not, Lever saw, with fear or anything like it. Jacky might run from a hostile crowd and Laver for one didn't blame him, but he wasn't afraid of a B.B.C. hack. He was shaking all right but not with fright; he was a very angry man indeed.

The picture in Laver's box blacked out.

Jacky struck the interviewer smartly, a solid backhander which broke his glasses. 'What the hell do you think you're doing? Inviting me here and playing silly buggers. You might have bloody killed me.'

Both cameras were dead as ducks but the sound went through the mixer and a middle-aged man was sitting at the control panel, mouth open, utterly fascinated. If Jacky had farted or mentioned the Queen he'd have faded him on a reflex as he'd promptly cut the fat woman at the first suggestion of slander. He had a good deal of experience and very precise instructions, but like all instructions from public corporations they were both punctiliously detailed and quite without inspiration. They certainly didn't cover this gorgeous stream of inspired abuse. The middle-aged man was shattered, frozen. Later, he realized, a shade admiring. The Anglo-Saxon words he knew, but in the bare five seconds before he pulled, Jacky had left the homespun far behind. He was on to the African English now, picturesque obscenities sometimes brutal and sometimes gay. He referred to the sexual act and several interesting variations of it. The interviewer had been born of them. He mentioned unclean matter which tellymen, he suspected, ate, unclean animals with whom this now broken hack was uncleanly familiar. Jacky could always talk fast and had.

The middle-aged man pulled the switch at last and Laver in Provost Road began to laugh. But not for long. What had happened in the studio he didn't yet know, but in his private estimation Jacky had moved from a civilized tolerance to something quite close to liking. But other people might not take that view—oh no. Five seconds at most he'd have said it had lasted, but five seconds had been enough and more. Enough for uncountable letters of protest, enough to destroy an evangelist once and for all.

Laver rang to Martin Dominy. 'Have you been watching telly?'

'I knew Jacky was on.'

'Can you guess what went wrong?'

'He jumped up and fell down. I doubt if he sat on a nail. When he got up again he looked genuinely shaken.'

'Find out, please.'

'Right.'

Laver's voice became more tentative. 'What do you think he was going to say?'

'From the context it sounded a perfect bomb. To me, that is. But you've got to remember I'm suspicious already. I've seen that file which Charles Russell opened and I've been poking about in Wiltshire. If I hadn't it mightn't have meant a thing.'

'Thank heaven he stopped or was stopped when he did. Do you think he has really got hold of something?'

'I don't know that.'

'Where do you think he got it from if he has?'

'From Mervin Seyer—we've got to face that.'

'Oh God.'

'Not Jacky's, please.'

'No . . .' Richard Laver said slowly: 'If Seyer slipped even a hint to Jacky—'

'Victor Lomax is around still. Very much so.'

5

Margaret Seyer and Peter Dinoba were walking in the garden which Richard Laver had approved of. She was delighted to see him, though he hadn't chosen the ideal moment for an unannounced call. Her father had been having one of his bad days, days when it was difficult to think of him as human. She had got him to sleep at last and was glad of company. Peter Dinoba might be of a different race but you could rely on him to be stimulating, much more so, she'd have admitted, than were many of her other friends.

He was watching her without seeming to, wondering if white men saw her quite as he did. In fact they did not. They saw a disturbingly beautiful woman but they saw the strong black eyebrows too, the jaw a shade too long for an English taste. Many men had desired her but few had ventured. Nefertiti, Princess of Egypt—one didn't risk it.

Peter was considering it and seriously.

He was asking her now: 'Were you watching telly yesterday evening?'

'Father was watching Jacky, of course. I wasn't really looking till . . .' She broke off the sentence, uncharacteristically embarrassed. Jacky D held her father, but in a different way he held Peter too, for he had given him back his Christian faith and Peter Dinoba blindly loved him for the gift. It didn't make modern sense but there it was. Perhaps Peter wasn't a modern man but she wouldn't hold that against him. Behind the Balliol voice, the better-than-comfortable job, behind the unconscious air of a man of the world, was Peter Dinoba, African.

But he was answering her easily. 'You may not have seen but at least you must have heard. Disastrous. Jacky has gone into hospital, by the way. We thought that best. The Committee is meeting tomorrow, you know, and we'll have to decide what to do, if we can.' He gave her his wide smile, then added: 'At least where he is he's protected from the journalists.'

'It *was* a bit of a shambles. What really happened?'

'I've seen him in hospital and naturally he's very upset. I doubt if he realizes quite what he said, but one thing he's perfectly clear about. He got an electric shock, a pretty severe one.'

'How could he?'

'Have you ever been in an interview room?'

She shook her head.

'I have, just once. You know my country struck diamonds some years ago. We're not xenophobic nor scared of neo-colonialism, so as we didn't know how to mine diamonds and far less market them, we licensed the concession to de Masseys. On very careful terms indeed. I'm Number Two at the London end.' He made a surprisingly English gesture of deprecation. 'I was lucky. Anyway, they wanted me to chat about it.'

'So you've seen the inside?'

'Just the once. And it isn't what you think at all. Watching the box it looks quite cosy but in fact it's a terrible muddle. You sit in what they call a Corner. The camera's right on top of you and the lights make you sweat in buckets. There's a tangle of wiring everywhere—'

'And one of them shorted on Jacky's chair?'

'Shorted,' he said, 'or was made to short.'

'You think it was deliberate?' She wasn't inclined to credit it.

'What *am* I to think? But somebody broke his last Rally up and they got away very professionally before the police could lay hands on a single one. You accept that as coincidence?'

'Like you I don't know. But why should anyone be

gunning for Jacky?'

He said as a question: 'To shut his mouth?'

'They didn't do that,' she said. She hadn't meant to.

'It's a pity they didn't. I was as astonished as anybody. I can understand it myself—he might have been killed—but there'll be plenty of others who won't. We'll know for certain tomorrow when the Committee makes its decision.'

It was her impression he was drawing back and she pinned him at once and sharply. 'But why should anyone want to shut his mouth?'

'He's a friend of your father,' Dinoba said slowly.

'And one of yours.'

'I'm not an eminent scientist, one whose work is, er, known.'

She guessed he had nearly said 'suspect' but had stopped himself; she didn't comment and he went on.

'Jacky was going to say something but now we're keeping the Press away from him.' He looked at her uncertainly but at last decided to take the chance. 'Could he have got some hint from your father?'

'I suppose he could—father often meanders. How much does it matter?'

'I really don't know.' He waved a hand at the down above them. 'We both know people who talk about that Establishment as though it were staffed by deliberate criminals, as though the Cabinet went down there alternate Mondays to gloat. But I don't believe that's what's wrong at all, I think the risk is exactly the opposite. There isn't enough control when the big things happen, and my hunch is that one is happening or has happened. Whatever it is it's dangerous, horrible.'

He was speaking, she thought, with an astonishing detachment; he'd said 'dangerous' and 'horrible' but he'd spoken almost calmly, as though he were white, of some major

49

Power, a man with hell on his doorstep and by now almost used to it. Not for the first time it was her impression he often forgot his race. He went on in the same cool tone.

'Will your father make it worse, do you think? By dropping more than some hint, something concrete and fatal?'

'You mean to Jacky?'

'Who else?'

'I don't think my father's gone far enough yet to spill anything really serious.'

'But he'd like to talk to Jacky. I can understand that.'

'You're perfectly right, father's miserable and burdened.'

'That's a danger—you must realize that. Suppose he got worse. . . .' They'd been strolling but he stopped suddenly. 'Margaret . . . It's not Jacky who scares me.'

'Who does?'

'Victor Lomax,' he said.

'You can tell me if you want to. I don't like him either.'

He hid a smile at the distaff logic. 'What do you make of him?'

'Very little except he's unexplained. What's a man like that doing on your Committee at all? Is he really even interested in what Jacky D preaches? He's a hard little business man . . .'

'Come clean,' he said, 'you must come clean.'

She hesitated: it sounded silly. There was everything and nothing. 'I've sometimes wondered,' she said uncertainly. 'He could be playing a hand of his own.'

'You're not the only one who has wondered.'

'Then shouldn't you be doing something?'

He raised his fine shoulders. 'But what?'

'Have you heard of the Security Executive? I've a relation who's the Head of it. I call him Uncle Richard—he doesn't like it.'

'He'd laugh at me if I went to him.'

'They never laugh at information. Of course it's up to you—you can think it over.' She'd been scribbling on a card and passed it across. 'That's his personal number.'

He put the card in his pocket. They'd stopped opposite a dark red rose and she stopped suddenly and picked it, holding it out simply, not spoiling the gesture with banal words. Dinoba put it in his buttonhole. He was enormously pleased and flattered but he too stayed silent. Against his old parquet skin the rose took a sudden and brilliant dignity. She hoped that he wouldn't spoil it by offering thanks. He did not. Instead he said conversationally:

'How's your father today?'

'Pretty bad, as it happens. You just can't tell. One day he's almost normal, the next he's hardly there.'

'There's this Committee meeting tomorrow morning and it's going to be vital for Jacky's future. We could use a sensible head, a tolerant man. Will he be up to it?'

'Your guess is as good as mine. You'll be fetching him of course?'

'We're sending a car.'

'Whose car?'

'Victor Lomax's. He offered first and we couldn't refuse.'

She didn't like it and said so.

'Not to distress yourself. I shall be coming too.'

'Suppose he objects.'

He looked at her. 'Let him object.'

'You sound pretty confident.'

'I can handle Victor Lomax.'

He probably could, she thought, and much else too. His quiet manner could be deceptive for she knew how he loathed the Establishment, but she wouldn't have thought the better of him if he'd ranted as some of her friends did, nor, much more personal, have enjoyed his company if he had. His call, his cool ways, had been balm to a day which had torn her nerves. She said without intending to:

'Suppose there was something up there really wicked.'

'It's frightening even to think about.'

'Do you think about it?'

'I try not to.' They began to walk to the gate and his waiting car. At it he took her hand and smiled. He looked down at the rose and said to it softly: 'I might be on the wrong end, you see.'

When he had gone she went back to the house. Her father was asleep still and she made herself supper and over it thought. When she had reached her decision she picked up the telephone.

'Uncle Richard?'

'I told you not to call me that.'

'Richard, then. Are you busy?'

'Not particularly.' He knew that about the Executive already. You could never afford to be too busy to listen.

'Then listen to me carefully, please.'

. . . She's had a trying day with that unhappy old man. Just the same she can be formidable.

'I'm listening.'

'Perhaps I'm wasting your time and perhaps I'm not.' She spoke for four minutes and Laver listened. At the end he said briefly:

'Thank you very much indeed.'

In his pay-bed in the hospital Jacky D was depressed but not yet miserable. The Committee was meeting next morning, and he was much too much the realist to be in doubt about it's decision. You couldn't sound off as he had done before a couple of million people and hope to live, not as a man of God, the rising evangelist. The Committee would cut its support off, drop him cold. So that would be the end of that, no white-robed choir of perhaps five hundred, no pealing organ, no Minister of the Crown to introduce him and puff his message, no Doctorate of Divinity from a university no one had heard of. He couldn't go back as a missionary, they were already sour and bitter that he'd left them for the Committee. Jacky D sighed enormously, wondering what dreadful job existed for an ex-missionary without academic or technical qualifications.

It was a daunting prospect and would have terrified most men. It frightened Jacky Dolan too but it didn't quite suppress him. He saw it that he was finished anyway, not so much by what he'd done as by what had clearly been done to him. A Rally had been broken up and that could hardly have been spontaneous, a live cable had caught his chair and made him swear. Which could have been a coincidence but Jacky Dolan didn't believe in them. So certainly he had enemies—that was enough: an evangelist with serious enemies hadn't a chance. Characteristically he hadn't too much considered who they might be. They existed and they were powerful, powerful enough to get him. Perhaps he'd offended some bigwig though he'd always been careful not to, or perhaps he'd just trodden on Catholic toes. In his bitter religious background the Bishop of Rome had been Bogeyman Number One. He could do anything and often did. Jacky wasn't very sophisticated.

Not sophisticated but resilient, and in its bizarre and unintended way a call by his wife had cheered him. It had certainly been fascinating to any student of human nature, the talk at one level, the thought at another. Jacky had run from a hostile crowd and Laver for one hadn't blamed him. Nor had Doris, or not in words, but she'd conveyed to him very expertly that she thought he was a worm, no man; he'd let the side down and failed in duty. He could hear the clichés forming as her pinched little mouth said other things. And as for his swearing bout, she hadn't brought herself to mention it. Her face had told him everything though, her personal horror and shame, her sense that he'd betrayed her. Not a word of reproof but equally none of sympathy. He'd been judged and found wanting. Now if it had been Anna, Anna Vescovi . . .

He sneaked a drink from the shoe-box where he'd hidden it. It had been brought by Victor Lomax and he'd never really cared for him, but he and Peter Dinoba were the only members of the Committee who had come to see him personally, and Lomax had guessed that he secretly liked a drink. In public he dare not since he was rabidly teetotal, but Lomax had guessed and had brought him a bottle. He'd hinted, too, at support at the next day's meeting. Jacky had thought that generous, though in fact it was simply necessary. If the Committee dissolved then Mervin Seyer would go with it, and with him Victor Lomax's contact.

Jacky drank a large whisky, half and half, relishing it happily. He wasn't finished, not quite yet. To start with he knew himself better now, much better than when he'd first returned to England. For instance he wasn't a physical hero, but he had something more important, he bounced back. Anna had taught him that, to roll with the punch.

Anna Vescovi—he'd need money.

He'd get it, he thought—no job as a clerk or a door-to-door salesman. He needed money so money would come. His private religion was by now a healthy paganism; he wasn't thinking of failings punished but of a run of bad luck which would surely end. It might indeed end when he came out of hospital. They'd been keeping the Press away from him and he'd realized and resented it, but they couldn't do that for ever. He had something to sell and he ought to sell it: the world ought to know of this terrible thing. And then let them try and get him again, whoever the bleeding bastards were! When a man was in the headlines he was safer than in a monastery. Richer too if he handled it properly.

As was often his habit Richard Laver was letting the other man talk and Martin Dominy was doing it more quickly than usual. 'It might all have been an accident and no one can show it wasn't. They had a stand-by camera—they always do. The working one went but it sometimes does, so the other cuts in automatically. It should have cut in, that is, if it hadn't shorted. Its cable shorted on Jacky's chair.'

'The sound?'

'They were sending live, not taping on video. The sound went on till another man cut it.'

'It did indeed,' Richard Laver said. 'Dolan was superb in his fatal way.' He rubbed his chin. 'That cable which shorted on Jacky's chair?'

'It hadn't been used for several days but they'd checked the insulation.'

'Passing it?'

'The electricians say so.'

'Anything on any of them?'

'They've all been there for years except one. Naturally he was questioned rather harder than the others, but none of them has been shaken. Insulation does go.'

'Has it happened before?'

'Oh yes, but they spotted it.'

'Do you believe it was an accident?'

'Not for a moment.'

'Then who fixed it?'

Martin Dominy said: 'Paul Frei.'

Richard Laver was astonished but concealed it very successfully. Martin Dominy had an excellent head and vastly more experience than his own. Laver said without irony: 'Perhaps there's a hole in the reasoning.'

'I don't flatter myself by calling it reasoning, but I'd like to start from Square One if I may. Are we agreed that Jacky D was going to blurt something?'

'It's a perfectly good hypothesis, especially as we've turned down accident.'

'Which he could only have got from Mervin Seyer, which shows that Mervin Seyer is even feebler than we thought.' Martin Dominy leant forward. 'Suppose Frei had feared that all along.'

'I'll suppose anything you invite me to.'

'Then the story makes a pattern, I think. Frei has this Victor Lomax who is trying to get something for him. Lomax can only get it from Seyer and has joined that Committee to make his contact. But the contact is wildly insecure, there's no guarantee he'll talk only to Lomax. He might equally talk to somebody else and perhaps he might do it before Lomax succeeded.'

'Jacky, for instance?'

'The old man dotes on Jacky, that's common knowledge.'

'Yes . . . The theory covers such facts as there are, but aren't you forgetting our Frei? If he'd been frightened of Jacky getting it first wouldn't he simply have had him removed? We know Paul Frei.'

'I'd thought of that too. They'd have killed him by now if they'd meant to do that, but killing has incidental risks which professionals try to avoid if they can. So they're destroying our Jacky as any sort of credible figure who could use information credibly. That Rally would have finished him if he hadn't been given a telly-spot. When on that he makes use of whatever old Seyer told him, or rather he tries to do so, but they'd been fearing that too so they shut him up. He swore fatally on top of it, but that was a bonus they couldn't have expected. Mr. Dolan, as Jacky D, is cooked. That would suit Paul Frei perfectly.'

'You're extremely persuasive,' Richard Laver said drily. 'May I bring you down to earth a bit?'

'I'm not the Great Detective, you know. I'd welcome something more concrete than theory.'

'Then if I'm following this correctly Victor Lomax is working for Frei. Working, moreover, on Mervin Seyer.' Laver's voice changed unexpectedly. '*But is he?* Have you checked on that side?'

'Yes, and I'm bound to admit it's negative. You've seen Lomax's file and it's what you'd expect. There are hundreds of Victor Lomaxes. Most of them wouldn't touch Frei with a pole but one or two might if they were crazy for money. The only pointer we have and it isn't more is that Lomax took some trouble to be elected to that Committee. As its only businessman he's pretty useful. He sees a lot of Seyer and he makes himself helpful with lifts in cars and so on. But I haven't any evidence that he's pressing Mervin Seyer.'

'No,' Laver said, 'but I have.'

'*What did you say?*'

'I told you before I was Seyer's distant cousin, though the connection with his daughter is a little more lively than distant. In fact she rang me a few hours ago. She is worried rather a lot, she said, since Lomax has been more pressing than you know. He has several times asked Seyer to dine but happily Mervin detests him. So, for that matter, does Margaret Seyer. He tries to sit next to the old man at meetings, he does a good deal more than just make himself useful. The Committee meets tomorrow to decide what to do about Jacky D and Lomax is driving to Seyer's house to bring him up to London and take him back.'

'Bad,' Dominy said. 'Alone?'

'I gather from Margaret Seyer not. There's another man on the Committee whom she trusts. He'll go with them too if he possibly can.'

'Which one is that?'

'Peter Dinoba.'

'The coloured one—we've made a dossier on him too. A Christian who lost his faith and recovered it from Jacky. Still hasn't seen through him, if there's anything to see beyond. Very good job in diamonds, very English. Upper class black if you'll let the phrase pass.'

'I will since it's accurate . . . So Lomax will be alone with Seyer unless Dinoba can somehow prevent it. What do we do?'

Dominy said promptly: 'We put a man on all of them, Lomax, Seyer, Dinoba, Jacky—the lot.'

Richard Laver sighed audibly. It was orthodox advice but he dare not take it. He reflected, then said gently: 'No. We're still on your guess about Lomax, though I happen to think it's probably right. But if Frei's in the background we're not dealing with amateurs, and the very best shadows sometimes get spotted. Four of them too . . . We can't afford to inhibit things. So put your man on Mervin Seyer, that's necessary for his own sake. But leave the others to give us a lead.'

'It's a risk, sir.'

'I accept it.'

Jacky had been confident and Lomax, with better reason, was more. He had it set at last, he really had. The last few weeks had been tedious and discouraging, hopeless approach work when Mervin Seyer clearly detested him, but tomorrow he'd have him alone and for several hours. In a car at that and the car was important. Seyer had smashed himself up in a car and he'd never been the same man since. He drivelled and he talked too much; he could be *made* to talk too much if you timed it right.

. . . Association of ideas and association of incident. They were the words of learned men and too often of quacks but Victor Lomax had faith in them. *They worked.* Mervin Seyer had had an accident . . .

He was going to have another.

6

The Committee was meeting in a flat in Lexham Gardens. The dining-room had been cleared for it and there were chairs round a rather fine pedestal table. The Field Marshal was at the head of it. Though it wasn't his flat and they hadn't voted for chairman he'd simply taken the place as his natural right. If he'd been smoking he'd have tapped the table with his pipe. But he only smoked in secret so he tapped with his square-cut nails instead.

'Ladies and gentlemen, fellow servants in the cause.' He could talk like that without a shiver. He ran an eye round the table: all present and correct. All but one, that is, and the one had been expected. His progressive Lordship had stayed away and the Field Marshal wasn't surprised at it. This was a sinking ship and every man knew it. The bishop, however, knew something else, he instinctively knew what to do about sinking ships. The Field Marshal grunted. Well, there was a proverb. Innocent of mixed metaphor he said aloud:

'If the cap fits wear it.'

'I beg your pardon?'

'Nothing. Please forget it. Where are we? Oh yes. That unfortunate affair on Thursday.'

Nobody spoke and the Field Marshal looked at them. He was more than a little dotty now but still had much experience of committees, foretelling with practised accuracy exactly how each man would vote . . . Jacky in or Jacky out? Drop him, get out from under? Or see it through? The Field Marshal looked round the table again. The two women do-gooders were foregone conclusions: their faces were glum and merciless, they'd send Jacky to the stake and worse and they'd pull the male do-gooder with them. Three. The two gentlemen from the country, charitable and decent men, would almost certainly abstain. Seyer seemed almost normal today, looking tired but entirely present, and Seyer ate out of Jacky's hand. The same went for that other one whose name the Field Marshal could never remember. He thought of him privately as the not-so-dark Darkie. He too was Jacky's *chela* and he'd follow him through thick and thin. Which was three to two with Lomax left, but the Field Marshal had little doubt about Victor Lomax. Victor Lomax was a businessman and in the world of business the one unforgivable sin was to tie the meeting, to throw it back to the chairman's vote. So Lomax would put his hand up last and when he saw it was three to two he'd make it four.

The Field Marshal nodded happily. He hadn't reached his exalted rank by taking awkward decisions unnecessarily.

'Once again, Ladies and Gentlemen. The decision before us is both unwelcome and inevitable. All of you were present at the last Rally, many of you will have been watching television on Thursday evening. These two regrettable incidents, these Factors for our Consideration—'

One of the women said: 'And there's a third.'

'Indeed?' The Field Marshal wasn't pleased. Staff Officers who brought up Factors which he hadn't himself thought of had seldom lasted long on his staff.

'Yes. He has relations with a woman not his wife.'

'You're sure?'

'I'm afraid I am.' She wasn't afraid, she was evidently relishing it, but she saw at once that she'd made a mistake. It was seven men to two women and she'd lined most of the men against her. None of them even looked at her but she could sense their quick hostility.

But Mervin Seyer was talking now, speaking in his quiet but still authoritative voice. He was very much on the ball today, the fine mind he'd been before his collapse, the brain trained to weigh facts levelly. 'You say you are sure, madam?'

'Perfectly.'

'You could swear to it?'

'I don't look through keyholes,' she said a little tartly.

'I did not suppose it.' Seyer was acid but still exquisitely courteous. 'I'm in no position to deny what you say, but let me put it another way. If this were a question of divorce, would you be able to give evidence?'

There was a silence. 'No, but my information—'

'Would, as hearsay, be inadmissible.'

Somebody said: 'Yes, indeed,' and it wasn't the other woman. One of the gentlemen from the country came alive. He was a Justice of the Peace and his sense of justice had been affronted. His face was rough from East Anglian winds, his voice was a little rougher. 'Tittle-tattle,' he said bleakly.

'I beg your pardon?'

'I do not withdraw.'

The Field Marshal took over quickly. 'Leaving this aside as I think we must . . .'

There was a murmur of assent but the Field Marshal wasn't happy. Now he wasn't so sure of the outcome, for that fool of a woman had put their backs up. The country gentlemen were simmering, their native feeling for fair play on edge; they'd vote all right now and they might vote wrong. The Field Marshal spoke to an uneasy silence.

'The decision we cannot avoid is this, and each must make it upon his conscience. In the light of the events which I do not propose to refer to again, do we continue to associate ourselves with Mr. Dolan? If I may put it more bluntly, do we continue to support him or do we not? I think we should all wish to be bound by the decision of the majority. I therefore call for a show of hands. For ending our relationship?'

Three hands went up, one male, two female.

. . . Those three, I'd expected them.

'For continuing it?'

There were three again promptly and the Field Marshal counted them—Seyer, Dinoba and Victor Lomax. He hadn't expected the last and it shook him. They were tied after all, he was on the spot.

He looked at the two countrymen but they paid him no attention. They were chatting together judicially. They might have been at their Quarter Sessions and quite possibly really thought they were. Finally both nodded and one rose. He put on a pair of spectacles, the sort round at the bottom and straight at the top. Over the straight part he stared at the female do-gooder. He was suddenly very formidable, centuries of decent dealing at his back.

'Despite the wholly disgraceful allegation—'

'How dare you!'

He ignored it contemptuously. 'In spite of the attempt to import scandal where it does not belong, my friend and I have reached a decision that our association with Mr. Dolan must be ended. We wish it recorded that we have done so with regret. That is all.'

He sat down.

The Field Marshal picked the threads up from the silence, looking at a note. 'He has three weeks to run on his present contract.'

'How much is that?' the Justice asked.

'A hundred and fifty pounds.'

'We should pay it.'

The male do-gooder said: 'I'll be damned—'

'I do not dispute it nor wish for another vote.' The magistrate pulled a cheque book from a pocket and wrote a cheque; he left it on the table without a comment.

The Field Marshal looked round for the final time. 'Have we finished?'

No one answered.

'Then I declare the meeting closed.'

The male do-gooder who owned the flat said: 'Coffee—'

'No, thank you.'

They trooped down to the street and their waiting cars and Richard Laver watched them climb into them.

It was entirely irregular that the head of the Executive should be actively concerned in what was called an operation. This he well knew and the convention was sound. His life, he supposed, was in its strange way valuable, and though he wore middle age with a notable ease and elegance one didn't invite humiliation in a rough house, far less tote guns on the very rare occasions when a servant of the Executive was even permitted to carry one. A man of forty would be an embarrassment to some younger man detailed to shield him. Not that the Executive fancied violence for its own sake: on the contrary it avoided it if it was possible to do so. Just occasionally it was not.

Richard Laver knew this and accepted it, but another tradition had brought him to Lexham Gardens. It was that the chair-borne commander soon went mad: worse, his troops soon learned to despise him. Besides, he told himself, conscious that he was stretching it, Mervin Seyer was a kinsman. He had married a Scot and had never regretted it.

So Richard Laver leant on the Garden railings, swinging his umbrella, smoking quietly, watching them come down from the flat, watching them drive their cars away. Mervin Seyer was last with Victor Lomax. His moment of sharp competence had left him, he was leaning on Lomax's arm looking grey and shaky. They got into Lomax's car: it began to move.

A dark man ran down the shallow steps quickly; he opened the door of the moving car, slipped in.

Laver smiled approvingly. It had been very well timed, very smooth and well planned.

On the opposite side of the road was a taxi with its flag down, apparently waiting. It began to move too but Laver held his umbrella up. The taxi stopped and he got in.

'Mr. Lightlove, I fancy.'

'That's me, sir. Good morning. The new gentleman, aren't you?'

'That's right. Mind if I take the ride?'

'A pleasure.'

'You'll have had your instructions already. Keep that Rolls in your sights.'

'She isn't much.'

But she was to Victor Lomax. His ambition was the latest Aston Martin. A status symbol? Certainly. He saw nothing amiss in symbols of status and one day, quite soon, he meant to have most of them. For the moment the Aston Martin was out but he wouldn't accept a substitute. A twelve-year-old Rolls had a cachet if nothing else.

As the two cars closed Richard Laver asked: 'Can you live with her if the driver plays tricks?'

Mr. Lightlove laughed. 'This isn't a regular taxi, sir.'

'I see.' Laver knew about this taxi though he'd never before driven in it. Its appearance was normal, police licence-plate and hire-flag: the engine, the chassis, the brakes were not.

They went over the Chiswick flyover and the car in front kept straight ahead. 'Odd,' Lightlove said.

'What's odd?'

'I know this is a motorway but it ends well north of the route to the Seyer house. Perhaps it saves you a bit of time. Or does it?'

'Keep going. And watch.'

'I've been watching. Can you see through their back window?'

'No.'

'I can't see a lot of myself but I see a bit. There seems to be a row going on. The driver keeps turning his head—very naughty. I think he's shouting at the coloured gent behind.'

'Can you see anything of Seyer?'

'He's sitting in the front seat, slumped down.'

'Is he wearing a safety belt?'

'No, I don't think so.'

'Is the driver?'

'He is.'

'I don't like it. Keep moving.'

Presently Lightlove spoke again. 'He's not going so fast but he's driving quite wickedly. Weaving in and out of the lanes . . . Christ Almighty.'

'I saw that one too. What do you make of it?'

'Lousy driving perhaps, but not if he does it again. No man does that twice in a day by accident.'

'Talking of accidents—'

Laver swallowed his heart as it happened again. He was certain now and he'd made up his mind.

'Can you force them off?'

'Not till he takes the slow side again. Then I'll push him into the halt-lane.'

'Without killing the lot of us?'

'I know my job,' Mr. Lightlove said.

'I believe you . . . Now.'

The car in front had pulled suddenly left and Lightlove put his foot down. The back of Laver's seat hit him squarely between the shoulders. His hat fell off and he picked it up.

In the prestigious old Rolls Victor Lomax was furious. No man jumped into a car like that just for the pleasure of taking a ride, and no man sat in the back like that, utterly silent, indifferent to abuse. What was the black bastard playing at? Victor Lomax considered a stop and throwing him off but he wasn't quite sure he could finish the job if he started. Dinoba wasn't a big man but he gave the impression that he could look after himself in a brawl. Besides, Seyer would notice and inevitably would ask questions. And Lomax didn't want Seyer asking questions; he wanted him answering them.

He ground his teeth but drove on. He'd have to play this one by ear and it was a difficult decision how much Dinoba's presence mattered. It was certainly a nuisance, not something which he had considered or would have accepted if he had, but when you stripped the leaves away you were left with an unwelcome witness, a nigger in the woodpile, or rather in the worn back seat. He couldn't interfere with you if you stuck to your original plan, he couldn't prevent an accident, though if he lost his head he might make it the sort which you hadn't intended. Very well, so you had your accident as planned. When a helplessly shaken Seyer would start to spill to you under pressure. Dinoba would certainly hear him too, but he wouldn't take in the half of it, while you yourself, who knew your trade, would get it all or all that mattered. And it wouldn't be fatal if this brute did hear a word or two. They weren't a people famous for their swift and decisive action. By the time he'd thought it over and made up his mind you yourself would have acted. You'd be out and away, the information with Frei in Amsterdam, a hundred thousand pounds of your own in a safe Swiss bank. You had never intended to stay in England.

So Victor Lomax drove on and he waited his chance. He wanted a jolting, not the sort of crash which would maim himself or Seyer. He looked sideways at Mervin Seyer, slumped in his seat. His head was on his chest and he was muttering inaudibly. The morning's moment of clarity had gone. And he hadn't put his seat belt on, nor had Lomax insisted there was one. Good. That made it easier.

Victor Lomax motored coolly on, looking for his accident. He was a good enough driver to make one, the sort of side-on scrape which shook severely but didn't kill. Twice he had almost had it but the others had been too fast for him. There'd been furious hootings, more furious faces, a shaken fist but no actual contact. If the Rolls had been ten miles faster then they wouldn't have had the legs of him.

He'd been noticing the taxi when he'd been looking in his mirror, and though he was driving fairly fast the taxi was keeping up with him. He was interested but no more, knowing that many London taxis had a good deal in hand which they didn't often use . . . Some damned tycoon on his way to the airport, promising the cabby a tenner if he'd make it to catch his plane . . .

Suddenly he saw his chance, the sort he'd been seeking but could never have guaranteed. There was a long clear stretch in the inside lane, then, almost a full mile ahead, a lorry in the middle one. He'd come up inside the lorry and it couldn't possibly get away when he edged the Rolls out.

He pulled into the inside lane, accelerating fiercely. He couldn't believe his wing mirror when the taxi came smoothly level. He looked at the speedometer—sixty-five and rising slowly. Too slowly. His foot was on the floor by now, the respectable old Rolls-Royce shuddering. Seventy and the taxi was there still. God damn the man, God damn his soul. There was a third fast car in the outer lane, the cabby was firmly blocked on his right. If he didn't brake soon he'd take the lorry up the backside.

By God, he wasn't going to. Instead his left hand was coming down and Lomax instinctively did the same. He wanted to have an accident, not have an accident forced on him. He put his left hand down but the taxi followed.

Christ, he's doing it again.

The taxi's bonnet was moving ahead. In the back was a tall man watching proceedings placidly. The driver's hand came down again . . .

Lomax was on the soft and braking hard. The back wheels broke outwards but the taxi had gone clear of him. He corrected efficiently but a shade too much. As he turned in towards the skid he caught another. This time the back of the Rolls went left. There was a crash as it took a wooden fence, the noise of a broken window, then a silence. Seyer's head had cracked the windscreen but he didn't seem to be bleeding; he was lying on the floor half supported by the door. Lomax reached across and opened it, and Mervin Seyer fell out on the grass.

Victor Lomax got down and went to him. Peter Dinoba was there already. From the taxi in front the tall man was climbing out fast.

Seyer was conscious but breathing shallowly, his eyes opened but unfocused. He said astonishingly:

'Jacky. I knew you'd come in the end.'

The tall man had joined them. Nobody uttered.

'Jacky, give me your hand.' The unfocused eyes were on Victor Lomax.

The tall man said softly: 'Give him your hand.' Lomax took Seyer's.

Peter Dinoba said: 'He's blind.'

The pale voice went on softly and they had to stoop to catch it. 'I trust you, Jacky. If only you'd let me tell you, save me.'

Lomax opened his mouth but shut it again.

'I need you, Jacky, I always have. I trust you.' There was a tautening silence while Seyer collected his strength, then the voice went on with the dreadful cunning of the senile. 'I really do trust you. Not like young Lomax—I've seen through *him*. But Jacky, I must tell you . . . Jacky . . . Jacky, save me.'

He gasped and his voice went weaker.

'Jacky, it's for black men. I think it is but I can't be quite sure. When I left it was black or yellow but I'm sure it was coming down black. Selective Pigmentation Disease and it does select. Just Asian plague to start with, then the chromosomes, you see, the pigmentation. Much more severe when we'd cultured it specifically. We worked it out on the genetic variations. There's some mathematics. I can't remember now but it'll come back . . .'

He was suddenly silent and Laver bent over him. 'He's alive still,' he said.

A police car was alongside now and the sergeant had come up to them. Laver showed him his pocket book and the sergeant looked at it hard and long. He then looked at Laver and finally saluted.

'What would you like me to do, sir?'

'Radio for an ambulance, please.'

'Right.' The sergeant signalled to his driver. 'Any particular hospital?'

'A nursing home—this one.' Laver scribbled on a visiting card. He wanted Seyer in a nursing home and it was important it be the right one.

The sergeant looked at Dinoba and Victor Lomax. 'And those two?'

'The African was a passenger, the driver showed poor judgement.'

'I see . . . Just an ordinary accident?'

'What else?'

'I'll have to take particulars, though.' Lightlove had joined them. 'Is that your cab?'

'Yes, not a scratch.'

'That makes it easier.' He was writing in a notebook as the ambulance came up to them. They put Seyer on a stretcher and the stretcher through the open door. Laver turned to the sergeant.

70

'And now can *I* help *you*?'

'I don't think so, sir, I'll do what's necessary.' He said 'necessary' in a tone which Laver recognized and appreciated, the tone of that quiet co-operation which the police would often give you if you played ball with them in turn. The Executive mostly did. It paid.

Laver looked at Peter Dinoba. 'Can I offer you a lift?' he asked.

Dinoba didn't answer him. He was staring, completely frozen. His world was in final ruins about his head.

Laver went back to Lightlove's taxi and Lightlove found a feeder and turned it round. As they drove back to London Richard Laver thought furiously, conscious of inexperience, trying to think as Charles Russell would have. He'd said he'd be available but on a Saturday he'd be happily golfing; he'd meet a commitment unquestioningly but he wouldn't much relish a summons back to London. Richard Laver smiled. He'd have to make his own mistakes and he'd have to learn the hard way. Russell would bail him out if they got too big.

. . . So Jacky D *had* known something and he'd been just about to blurt it when Frei had stopped him. That was Dominy's hypothesis and Richard Laver hadn't a better one. Not that Jacky was principal danger now: he'd been in hospital for nearly two days and no newspaper had even the hint of a story beyond the facts that there'd been an accident and he'd sworn viciously. They were running that as they'd run the Rally, deadpan, contemptuously, or simply as low comedy. That meant that if he'd had some message he hadn't yet delivered it, which wasn't perhaps surprising since an embarrassed Committee had promptly delivered him into a hospital where no doubt they'd be trying to fend off the Press. So far, it seemed, they'd completely succeeded, but they couldn't hold that line for ever. When Jacky came out of hospital he'd be perfectly free to talk as he pleased.

The Executive would have to meet that as it came, and it might not have to meet it at all: what it might be facing could be sensationally more serious. Sensationally, Richard Laver decided, was the word and alas the right one. Jacky Dolan mightn't have known very much, just the name perhaps and a little more. S.P.D.—Selective Pigmentation Disease. Any newspaper would have made something of that, but four men now knew much more than the name and two of them weren't officials. They knew what it selected on, which was black men, black men, black men, and one of the two was working for Frei or if he were not then his actions were inexplicable. Richard Laver swore. And he'd been worrying about the newspapers!

He began to tick the people off . . . Mervin Seyer? He'd put him in a nursing home which he'd inherited with Russell's chair. It was rather a special nursing home, you couldn't go browbeating Seyer there, far less try forcing your way in with guns. So Seyer was safe for a time which was something . . . Lomax? Laver would have to talk to Lomax. He might easily refuse to attend but Dominy was a persuasive man and Laver would send him to do his best. That evening . . . Peter Dinoba?

Dinoba was black and he'd heard too much, too much for a man already suspicious. He was black and he was educated. He'd looked utterly shattered, completely broken.

Peter Dinoba was going to be tricky.

7

It was nearly noon and he was still on his bed unshaven, something he hadn't failed to do since he'd come to England six years ago. His hands were behind his head but he wasn't relaxed: on the contrary he was as taut as a drum and feeling as brutally beaten. He was trying to get his thoughts straight but they wouldn't begin to form for him, only flashes and snatches not always in order, a kaleidoscope of the life which had come to him unexpectedly.

. . . Childhood—it had been happy. His father had been immensely old, almost forty when he'd been born to him, but his mother had been a junior wife, a favourite too and he'd seen much of his father. To the child he'd seemed enormous, almost godlike in his spotless robes, but he'd been kind and just and often playful. There had been brothers almost old enough to have fathered him if they'd wished to, but also a swarm of cousins and kinsmen to play with in the garden's dust. It had been hot, he remembered, dry hot in the summer, almost cool in the winter evenings. Once he'd touched his father's car in the dawn and the static had knocked him flat on his back. He had thought it was some spirit and run weeping to his mother. His mother couldn't explain to him but a half-brother had done his best. It had been hot and healthy, a climate for men, not like the humid heat of the Coast, the land of the black men, the less than slaves. He'd been astonished when they sent him there, a homesick and at first resentful boy.

. . . Boyhood—that hadn't been easy. They'd treated him well at the Mission school and in the holidays he always went home, but he'd been nearly fifteen, a full-grown man, before he'd realized why he'd been sent to this strange school. He'd imagined the solemn conclave of his father and of his courtiers. They couldn't go on like this, they really couldn't. Those damned coastboys were everywhere. One went into a Post Office and there was a monkey face behind the grille; one tried to buy a few sacks of seed, the sort which the government recommended, and there was a black black hand held out for its shameless cut. The pigs were everywhere—clerks, minor civil servants, shopkeepers, everywhere but in gentlemen's work, which to his father and his yeomen meant the police force, farming, the army. And one couldn't go on dealing with them in the time-honoured, simple, ageless way, one couldn't go on slapping them down, chopping their ugly nuts off if the beating wasn't effective. Why, the animals had the law on you, an alien law at that, a foreigner's code. The greybeards had thought it scandalous, as did many men whose beards weren't grey. Books were certainly of the devil, but since the coastboys exploited book-learning you'd have to meet them on their own bad ground. It was distasteful and maybe dangerous but the writing was on the wall for all to read. Unhappily not many could. So every family which could afford it must forthwith choose its brightest son. Then down to the Coast he must go to a Mission school.

The Mission school had been mixed experience. He had come with some English to start with but not an African word in common with the majority of the other boys. He hadn't liked them either, they hadn't been honest, they lied and stole. They smelt. But one thing he'd had, he'd been bright as a pin, and his teachers, like all good ones, had given him more the more he took. He'd sailed through every local exam, then won a place at Oxford, no less. He'd almost got a scholarship too, his father was proud and delighted. If only he hadn't apostatized.

He moved on his bed uneasily. He had to be fair and his father had not been, assuming at once that the missionaries had got at him. In fact they'd been wholly scrupulous, for his school was an old one and liberal too, a hundred miles both in ethos and style from the dubious hot-gospellers who employed Jacky D. It hadn't been as his father had thought, they hadn't tried to nobble him: it had happened accidentally, the flash on the Damascus Road. His teachers were teachers first and the best ones brilliant, but there was a tradition in their Society that they shouldn't decline into pedagogues in ivory towers. They did other work outside their schools and some of it was very tough.

He stirred again, smoking fiercely. So one night he'd gone out with one of them, begging it as a treat, receiving a smile. They had walked to a hut where a child was dying and he'd been horrified as he'd never been. Not at death, he'd seen plenty, but at the squalor, the stink. The hut was a cesspit, in his own country they'd have razed it. Inside a child was dying but the stench . . . His teacher had held out his hand but he couldn't take it; instead he'd stayed outside the hut, vomiting uncontrollably.

But his teacher had gone straight in and that was that. This religion was good. Just *good*. It made saints of men. The doctrine hadn't troubled him, he'd simply listened and accepted it. All religions had to have one.

His father had been furious but he hadn't quite made the final break. Peter Dinoba realized that his father hadn't dared to. There was far too much family money sunk in himself; he was educated now, an asset. So his father hadn't cut him off but had let him go on to Oxford.

. . . Oxford and total happiness, marred by a single streak of unease. He remembered the happiness gratefully. He'd been good at his books and a very fair bat in college cricket; he hadn't sought his own kind nor shunned it either, for he'd been accepted and assimilated, not as of another race but simply as a good college man. But he hadn't been wholly happy when he realized that he'd lost his faith. Perhaps, he thought now, that put it crudely, for he'd never been much of a Christian in the sense that the dogma had held him. He'd wished simply to join a community which he'd admired with a boy's quick passion, and now he no longer admired it he'd felt lost and indeed betrayed. He couldn't live without a background, his race and blood made that unthinkable, so he'd looked for three days at something called humanism and he'd looked for a year at the Marxist faith without ever quite succumbing to it. And then one day he'd gone to Jacky's and Jacky had given it back to him, the sense of belonging, of common roots. He was perfectly conscious that Jacky had since exploited him, putting him on that Committee of his, using his colour as bait for others. Come to think of it he'd been Jacky's dog, but there was nothing discreditable in being a dog. A working dog in the right sort of household had his place. He belonged to a community.

Peter Dinoba had been whole again, content.

And now it was dust and ashes, a bitter burn. Damn them, damn them, damn them. Damn Jacky, damn Lomax, all of them. God damn the way they took you in, God damn the way they dropped you out. You could live for a year without thought for your colour, you could even admire their women, accept their rose. Then the mirage vanished suddenly, you were naked and cold in the desert dawn. The fine friends in de Masseys which you'd chosen instead of diplomacy, your casual English contacts who called you Pete, Margaret Seyer, this way of life.

It was white and you were not. Selective Pigmentation Disease . . . He still didn't quite credit the words he'd heard, but with an effort he made himself think of them coolly. 'Jacky, it's for black men. Selective Pigmentation Disease and it does select. Just Asian plague to start with. We worked it out on the genetic variations.'

Peter pulled himself off his bed and bathed and shaved. In his bath he began to think again, not quite logically but practically. Mervin Seyer had talked and Lomax had meant him to. You must start from that. Then from Lomax's point of view any plan had gone off at half cock: Seyer had talked but not enough and there'd been unexpected witnesses. One had been himself, mistrusting Lomax, the other a tall man with an air of assured authority; he hadn't acted like a policeman but a sergeant of police had saluted and taken his orders. His presence had been coincidence? That would be somewhat stretching it since the tall man's car had clearly forced them off the motorway and Margaret had once told him she had a cousin in the Executive. Dinoba hadn't been to it but there'd been nothing to stop her doing so. He wouldn't blame her if she had since it was proper to use one's family.

He climbed from the bath and dried himself. In any case he wasn't worried about the tall man. If the tall man was an official, and it was a very fair guess he must be that, then he'd certainly keep what he'd heard to himself, and even if he wasn't one he hadn't the air of an idle talker. Victor Lomax on the other hand . . .

Lomax was different. Victor wouldn't chatter either but he would use. He'd come on Jacky D's Committee and he wasn't the type to want to; he'd been stalking Mervin Seyer and he'd fixed it to drive him home alone; his firm made complex chemicals and he'd heard 'Asian plague' and 'genetic variations'. Bad enough in that Establishment, wicked, unthinkably evil. But out in the cold commercial world the unthinkable often happened. Peter Dinoba knew for he worked in diamonds.

He looked at his watch, astonished that it was afternoon. He realized he hadn't eaten all day but he was much too tense for appetite. He'd have to talk to Lomax who'd be

77   DD—F

back in his flat by seven at the latest. That gave him three or four hours to think if he could, but he knew that the time would be wasted. He wasn't capable of serious thought, nor of forming any logical plan through the fog of his fear and his personal shame. Fear for the future, shame for the past. They'd horned him, he'd worn them willingly. Damn them, damn them, damn them. They were all the same, they were not his people. Those animals on that stinking Coast were nearer to him than these pitiless whites.

He made himself scrambled eggs and somehow ate them. He hadn't a plan nor the will to make one. He'd simply go round to Lomax's flat where what was written upon his forehead would be fulfilled.

At a quarter to seven he found a taxi.

Jacky D. had discharged himself early that evening, for he was restless and bored in hospital, aware that he wasn't really sick, simply put where he was for the convenience of his Committee, whose decision had been communicated to him along with the cheque for a hundred and fifty. He'd been grateful for that, it would come in useful, but it wasn't the sort of money he needed.

Within half an hour he had made his contact and the *Gong* had sent round a write-up man. The write-up man had been clearly excited but one thing he had insisted on: Mr. Dolan had suffered certain, well, setbacks, his credibility wasn't quite what it had been, so it might be essential to name his source. Perhaps that would be the second stage of what was going to be a story to run for days. The write-up man would speak to his editor. Moreover the powers-that-be would kick, and the only way to answer that was to name Mervin Seyer. Or perhaps it would be enough if they simply threatened to. It didn't really matter that there hadn't been any witnesses when Seyer had talked about S.P.D. The background was known and it stood by itself. Mervin Seyer was known to be gently ga-ga and Mervin Seyer was Jacky's follower. He'd even been on that Committee of his. Let Whitehall choke on that if they started to get absurd ideas, for instance a D Notice, though somewhat belated, or pressure behind the scenes—all that. They often tried it on and the *Gong* didn't like it.

So Jacky and the write-up man had made their little arrangement easily. Only the terms were outstanding still for Jacky had pitched his figure high. The write-up man said he couldn't meet it but that didn't mean his paper wouldn't, so he'd go and ask them straightaway and ring back with the decision. Then on Sunday morning they'd talk again, and there it would be on Monday morning, slap on Page One and God help Whitehall.

The *Gong* took a taxi back to Fleet Street and Jacky picked up the evening paper. It was the latest edition which the write-up man had left behind. Jacky looked at it idly. Such political news as it carried bored him, he didn't race. On the front page, down on the right-hand side, was a quarter column. He read it once without taking it in, then suddenly he was trembling. A Mr. Victor Lomax had been found dead in his Onslow Gardens flat. He'd been a director of Farrell and Haye and had been closely associated with the evangelist Jacky Dolan. There had been violence, firearms, a strangling. The police were treating it as murder.

Jacky's hands shook so much he could hardly read. . . . The Rally, that affair at Wood Lane. So they hadn't just been some bigwig whom he'd offended, some sect whose toes he'd trodden on. Bigwigs didn't murder people, religious denominations strangle. This was serious, deadly. He couldn't think why yet and far less how, but Lomax was dead and Jacky wasn't. Not yet. But if he talked to the *Gong* and let them splash it . . .

He was every bit as frightened as he'd been at the Rally which started it, far more frightened than at Wood Lane. He had a little of Lomax's whisky left and he poured a shot and gulped it. Then he telephoned to Fleet Street. Mr. Dolan had changed his mind. No deal.

Several miles to the south of him Martin Dominy, though not frightened, had been astonished. At a quarter to seven Peter Dinoba had found his taxi, and at a quarter past eight Dominy's Alfa had been nosing its way into Onslow Gardens, driving slowly along the western side. Martin Dominy knew the number but not exactly where to find it. Unexpectedly he accelerated. Outside Lomax's tartily painted front door were two police cars and an ambulance.

Dominy pulled his hat down hard and drove away.

8

Victor Lomax hadn't been expecting a visit from Peter
Dinoba or indeed from anyone else. He was spending the
whole evening in since he was hoping for a telephone call;
he had reported to Paul Frei's Striped Tie though not
knowing him by Frei's private name, and his report had
been acknowledged and nothing more. Now he was waiting
for further orders, at least for a word that he'd made some
progress. Peter Dinoba too was awaiting events. For his race
he wasn't emotional but this evening he wasn't thinking at
all, simply feeling and feeling deeply. He'd have to go to
Lomax and they'd have to have the matter out. The gods—
he didn't care which—would decide the issue.

Lomax hadn't wished for company but he couldn't refuse
him entry. When he had him in an armchair he asked:

'May I offer you a drink?'

'No thank you, I don't drink.' Peter had spoken instinctively, not intending what had become untrue. In fact he'd
been drinking for several years though only in a social way.
There was nothing in Christianity which forbade it. Now,
on a reflex, he simply said he didn't drink. Not that he
wished to drink with Victor Lomax. No indeed.

'You don't mind if I do?'

'No.'

Dinoba looked at Lomax curiously. He was a fair way
from being drunk yet but it was clear he had had a drink or
two, the three or four drinks at the end of the day which so
many of these strange barbarians took. Alone. Pretending it
was a medicine. Odd.

Lomax said easily: 'Tell me what I can do for you."

'You can tell me your interest in S.P.D.'

'Selective Pigmentation Disease? What old Seyer started
to babble about? What makes you think I've an interest?

Assuming the thing exists, that is.'

'A fair question—I'll tell you. First you've been scratching acquaintance with Mervin Seyer. I put it crudely because it's shortest. Then you fixed it to drive him home alone and I believe you meant to shake him up. If you shook him enough he might start to talk—'

'I've been wondering why you jumped my car and you're jumping something else, you know. You're jumping to conclusions too.'

'I may be jumping to the wrong one. I hope I am.'

'It's the wildest idea I've ever heard.'

'It would be if you sold motor cars.'

Lomax laughed—it was a good one. It wasn't over-amused or forced but the laugh of a man who was still at ease. 'If you hadn't told me you didn't drink . . .'

He left the sentence to float and Dinoba waited. He looked at Victor Lomax again and he looked at Lomax's living-room. He might not be thinking logically but his observation was unimpaired. He had never visited Lomax before and this room confirmed much he had only guessed. The furniture was modern, Swedish, the pictures were abstracts and to an African eye quite meaningless. There'd been money spent here and quite a lot but it had gone on a shell not a room to live in, some decorator's idea of the rising young executive's pad. Well, if that was how Lomax chose to live it wasn't Dinoba's business.

He stiffened unexpectedly. On the mantelshelf were three carvings and he recognized them at once. From the Coast of course, and rather good. But they were idols, an outrage: he ought to smash them as an offence to God. He hadn't thought much about idols in recent years. Now he was horri-fied, hundreds of years of belief and training shocked and ashamed by this pagan display. At home they'd burn the house down too.

82

But Lomax's manner had suddenly changed. He had realized he was on dangerous ground and a counter-attack seemed the best way off it; he said angrily: 'So you think I've been spying on Mervin Seyer.'

'It's an explanation of what's happened.'

'Then you owe me an apology.'

He saw at once that he'd made a mistake. The words had been a formula, something intended to wrong-foot this African. But he wasn't taking them as a formula, he was taking them as a literal demand. So Lomax had asked an apology and he wasn't going to get it. Dinoba was sitting silently, for the first time faintly smiling. Hell. Lomax was committed now, he couldn't back down, he couldn't just laugh and shrug it off. Not with a black man. Never.

Dinoba didn't answer him, he knew exactly where he stood now. To Peter Dinoba, African, Lomax had never seemed quite a gentleman. Now he was sure of it. No gentleman asked for apologies. From a source where they'd be valuable they'd be offered perfectly freely and from any other sort of man they weren't worth the tongue which spoke them. But Lomax had made a demand and now was stuck. Doubly stuck. For Peter had no illusions about what Lomax would privately think of him. He knew the type and avoided it: they weren't his friends. To the Lomaxes of a shrinking world Peter was simply inferior. Lomax would have a word for him, that hideous disyllable, the basic insult. Fine. For you couldn't demand of a nigger and let it go. Lomax would have to do something, this was the break. Peter Dinoba waited.

So did Lomax. If Peter hadn't smiled at him he'd have been tempted to swallow his background and let it go, but that handsome smiling face, this superior coon . . .

He finished his fourth whisky and then stood up. He slapped Peter Dinoba's face.

Dinoba rose too but he didn't strike back. Instead he took Lomax's nose and tweaked it hard. It was a punishment for servants and he knew how to do it perfectly. It hurt quite surprisingly.

Lomax, eyes watering, started to hit at once. He hit as he'd been taught to at the school he was rather ashamed of, entirely forgetting another lesson, that you couldn't hurt niggers by thumping their heads. He poked out a stream of snappy lefts, a string of right crosses more effective if they'd been crossing anything. For Dinoba would have no part of this. He took one or two punches, then ducked quickly below them; he took Lomax's knees and he pulled at them smoothly, smoothly but hard and very high. Lomax's head hit the carpet before his bottom. He lay there winded helplessly, a trickle of whisky and soda from the corner of his open mouth. His legs were apart and for a second Peter hesitated. A single good kick would do it.

He shook his head. He wanted Lomax talking, not in agony and crippled. He pulled him up almost casually, dumping him back on the ugly armchair.

Lomax was getting his breath back slowly, reaching at last for the whisky, greedily pouring.

'Not so much of the hard stuff, I want you sober.'

'It's my whisky, damn you.'

'One then—just that.' Peter was holding the reins now and knew it.

Victor Lomax was thinking. He'd thought in his car that Dinoba would be competent in a brawl, noticing the deep flat chest, the look and the air of a martial race. Very well, so he'd been right in that; now he'd trapped himself in a bad mistake and he'd have to recover decisively. For that he needed time and for time he'd talk. Oh yes, he'd talk, he'd talk fast and plenty. There was a gun in his desk and he meant to reach it. When he had himself under control he said:

'You've got it half right but only half.'

'You mean you *were* after S.P.D.? From Mervin Seyer?'

'Yes.' (The man's guessed that anyway.) 'But it wasn't what you might think. My firm—'

'What about your firm?'

'They're Quakers. Think for yourself.'

'I'd rather you told me. Quickly.'

Victor Lomax moved his shoulders though it hurt. He was an excellent salesman which meant that he was a fair actor too, so he said reasonably, persuasively: 'If S.P.D.'s what they say it is it's the most terrible thing in a terrible world. Quakers aren't fools and they've very tender consciences. They wanted to get the antidote, assuming, that is, there is one. I wanted to help—that's all.' He was candid, impressively man-to-man. 'Work it out for yourself as I told you to. You're on the wrong end of S.P.D. yourself. So which way would you rather have it? S.P.D. in the hands of governments, and it wouldn't be only my own, you know— the antidote too if they've managed to find one—or S.P.D. in the hands of governments but the antidote with a private firm, god-fearing, peace-loving decent men?'

Dinoba was silent and Lomax went on watching him. He'd made another mistake though he didn't know it; he'd made Peter Dinoba think again and he was doing so deliberately. Peter said at last:

'No.'

'No what?'

'No truth. It's clever of course, but it doesn't jell. No private firm ever thought like that.'

'Mine does. They're Friends. I told you.'

'I don't care what church they go to, not a bit. I'm in

85

business myself. Remember that—diamonds. Commercial espionage is common form but no private firm goes for government secrets. Not that sort, at least—not S.P.D. They might stumble on it by accident but they'd be frightened out of their wits if they did. As for playing about with an antidote, that's a stupid lie.'

'I assure you you're wrong,' Victor Lomax said. He was hoping he sounded persuasive still.

'No, I'm not wrong, I've got it now. It fits. You've made it fit.' Peter stood up but he didn't come closer. 'You weren't working for your firm at all but you did have something behind you. A government or perhaps just a man. And now you're going to tell me.'

'You're dreaming things.'

'We'll soon find out.'

He took two paces forward and stood over Lomax. Victor Lomax had been waiting for it. He didn't get up but he bent his knees and the two-footed kick sent Dinoba sprawling.

When he got up he was looking at a pistol. He knew a little of firearms and he saw that it wasn't a big one. A shot in the head would kill him just the same. Lomax was saying gratingly:

'And now we'll talk. Sit down.'

'I prefer to stand.'

'Sit down, you black bastard. Down.'

Peter Dinoba flushed but he didn't move.

'Sit, nigger. Sit.'

Peter was on him too fast for aim but he fired as he staggered off balance. A knee came up hard and Lomax gasped, but he was holding the pistol still as he fell. He fired again as Dinoba followed him down.

Ten minutes later Dinoba left Lomax's. Three things had just happened and none had ever happened to him before. First he'd been called a nigger and that was enough.

86

Secondly he'd been shot at twice and one bullet was still in his forearm. Thirdly he had strangled a man and he hadn't intended to do so. He'd been seized by an enormous rage, the reverse of what some whites felt for many Africans. So he'd suddenly been in frustrated fury, not especially against Lomax but against this pretentious race of white incompetents. Why, they couldn't get a damned thing right! They shook a half-mad old man to bits, then got from him only a clue to his secret; they told you stupid lies which exposed the truth; they pulled guns on you but they didn't kill. There wasn't a thing you could do with them. Nothing.

He looked at his arm as he eased it into his overcoat. He was going to need a doctor.

9

Paul Frei was in a Turkish Bath. He had been through the hot rooms and now lay on a chaste mattress under massage. A vast Swedish girl was doing it, and in any other circumstances it would be described as a brutal beating. Frei suffered it uncomplainingly for he had weight to lose and he knew about Swedes. The girl probably wasn't an active sadist but she'd cordially detest his guts; she'd envy him for his wealth and power, she'd despise his ugly and ageing frame. It wasn't pretty and he knew it but he suffered that uncomplainingly too. Such sex as he needed he simply bought.

The girl finished at last with a thunderous slap, a gesture of barely concealed contempt. Paul Frei ignored it blandly— she knew her job. He could have bought the Bath and had her sacked but she was an excellent masseuse, entitled to her Nordic spleen. Besides, the Bath lost money: he knew that too as he knew most things in Amsterdam. He took his cold plunge and a bath robe from an attendant. Matches and his cigar case had been put into the pocket. Then he went to a bare cubicle and lay down on the bed and thought. He always thought well in a Turkish Bath.

. . . That report which Striped Tie had sent on from Victor Lomax. It was useless. In any matter of science there was always a crisis one way or the other and Lomax had told him only that it was past. So it had come down for Blacks and that wasn't enough. There was always a point of balance, heads or tails.

Or life or death. Frei knew that from experience.

He lit a cigar and looked at his watch. He could afford ten minutes of reverie. The pictures began to form in the fine pale smoke.

. . . North Africa. Oberst the Baron Paul von Frei, a Staff

Colonel on an illustrious staff. His headquarters had lagered one night and the bombers had caught it. They hadn't quite wiped it out for the flak had been good, and the English had been unlucky too. One bomb had dropped a few yards from his General's caravan, a dud. His General had come out and stared. No, he wouldn't move his caravan, not with shaken men watching him. The colonel would have it defused at once. Arrange it.

He had arranged it or had thought he had, but when the Captain of Engineers arrived von Frei knew at once that the man was finished. Courage was expendable—an American had said that but it was true—and this unfortunate Captain of Engineers had drawn his last cheque on a closed account. Frei hadn't despised him that he wouldn't face the job, or not alone; he was a brave man himself, not a lunatic hero, which meant that he'd often been very scared. Discipline, so far, had always held, discipline and tradition too, but this Engineer Captain had gone far beyond either. He had medals and he had earned them; he had earned them too hardly.

So the pair of them had crawled up to the bomb, hard Junker baron and a nobody from the Rhineland. The Captain had had a box of tricks and he'd listened in its earphones, turning the dials. Then he'd shrugged and von Frei had known. The Captain was scared but he was also at a total loss. This wasn't a type of bomb he'd seen before.

Paul von Frei had considered it. The orthodox course was to clear the lager but he knew that his General would never wear it. This wasn't simply stubbornness, a personal pride or a false panache: his men had been taking a beating, and in this sort of warfare morale was paramount. Morale meant example first and all the time, so his General was now in his caravan though Frei doubted he was sleeping again. It was certain he wouldn't consent to move. Von Frei nudged the

Captain—he hadn't retreated. But nor did he move when Paul von Frei touched him. Frei saw he was weeping quietly.

Oberst the Baron von Frei inched forward. He had the Engineer Captain's tools but little knowledge of their use. There was a plate on one side of the bomb and Frei stared at it, collecting himself. Then he clumsily unscrewed the nuts, not ashamed that his hands were shaking. Inside was a larger hexagon nut. The fuse.

. . . Was it left-hand thread or was it right? He didn't know which and nor did the Captain. So turn your wrist one way and you lived to remember the story in this comfortable Turkish Bath. Turn it the other . . .

Odd that he couldn't remember which way he'd turned. After four turns he knew he'd won.

His General had been delighted with the Captain of Engineers. Typically Frei had slipped away. Staff Colonels defusing bombs meant a strict inquiry, and Frei, a professional soldier, loathed them.

He let the day-dream fade reluctantly. And thinking about his General, there was a maxim about generals: you dismissed the unlucky ones. And not only generals, unlucky servants, and Victor Lomax had been unlucky. He hadn't been unintelligent, getting on that Committee had been a sound enough first move, and the plan to make Mervin Seyer talk had had the merit of simplicity. And what had Lomax got for it? Almost nothing. Selective Pigmentation Disease, but that was only a popular tag for something Paul Frei had long suspected. It would be used against black skins which was something more, but alone was worth little or nothing . . . 'Just Asian plague to start with, then the chromosomes, you see, the pigmentation. Much more severe when we'd cultured it specifically. We worked it out on the genetic variations.'

Tantalizing, infuriating. So near to success and so far from it in the final result. For just as old Seyer had started to talk he'd lost consciousness and they'd taken him off. Bad luck on Victor Lomax no doubt, but bad luck was extremely dangerous. Now Lomax was dead and that settled it for you, otherwise you'd simply have had to cut him as a loss. Even if he'd lived he would now be useless since he couldn't have got near Seyer again. That much was certain.

But he hadn't just died, he'd been killed and that was curious. Striped Tie had sent a report on that too, but he hadn't known the killer nor ventured comment. Still, a fourth man had been present at Seyer's collapse though Lomax hadn't noticed him much. He'd been tall with an air of authority—there were thousands like him. A man from the Executive, even this new man of theirs in person? It was conceivable—Striped Tie had feared their intervention. And if the Executive had been present had it also arranged for Lomax to die? Paul Frei shook his head for that would strongly suggest the amateur. The Executive could be ruthless, even deadly where its duty lay, but it had the distaste of all good officials for breaking butterflies on the wheel. They'd have had plenty of ways of dealing with Lomax short of sending a man to murder him. Besides, to kill him would be pointless—just one man. There'd been a second present when Seyer had talked, a Negro called Peter Dinoba who was alive.

A Negro, that was significant. He'd been on Jacky D's Committee and he'd jumped into Lomax's car unasked . . . Unexplained and as such disturbing. And he'd heard what Seyer had said about S.P.D. S.P.D. was for black men, Dinoba was black.

Paul Frei made a mental note of it since he seldom made a written one. He'd be obliged to change his plan to get S.P.D. but it was still the first rule that you minimized your risks. This Dinoba would have to be watched and maybe more.

He pulled evenly on his long cigar. It was easy to talk of changing one's plans, of the virtue of flexibility, and he hadn't reached where he stood today by backing lost causes obstinately. No, you cut your bad bets but ran the good ones to the limit, so you'd have dropped Victor Lomax if he hadn't been removed for you. But now you had to find another tool. Not so simple, even difficult. The Executive hadn't killed Lomax but almost certainly was alerted; Mervin Seyer was in a nursing home, a very sick man and for all you knew dying.

Then you took what the gods had offered and if you handled it well they'd pull for you. Frei had always thought of Jacky D as a possible second string if Lomax failed, a man who might serve him if once he had motive, and now he had that motive, money, since he was finished in his repellent trade. Motive and more—he had means, opportunity.

Mervin Seyer had taken Lomax's hand but he'd thought he was talking to Jacky D.

Paul Frei swung his legs down, ringing the bell, and a valet brought his clothes in and he dressed himself meticulously. Then he drove back to his office in the big but austere Mercedes. There he gave his orders crisply and his secretary confirmed a flight. Half an hour later a packed travelling bag was brought in to him and an hour and a half later still he was talking to Striped Tie again, speaking as he always spoke, a sharp flow of orders in almost perfect but stilted English. But at the end he asked untypically:

'Do you consider this new plan will work?'

'I can do as you ask, I can talk to Dolan. But I'm not going near that nursing home, not a home with a private line to the Executive.'

'That is a complication, yes.'

'One fatal for me but not necessarily for Dolan.'

'So it seems to depend on Mr. Dolan's need of money.'

'Which I know to be pretty desperate. His Committee has discharged him and he can't go back to Africa. He's snarled up with another woman.' Striped Tie looked up inquiringly. 'A hundred thousand pounds, I think you said.'

'The same as I promised Lomax—why not? The same work, the same object.'

'A down payment might swing him.'

'Which he could pocket and then do nothing.'

'True.'

'You think it is really worth the risk? I am asking your expert opinion.'

'Yes.'

Paul Frei said: 'Fifty thousand pounds. One half.' He had many and serious vices but pettiness wasn't one of them. He reflected, then asked a question again. Striped Tie had known him ask one but never two.

'If this man accepts my terms can he hope to get to Seyer?'

Striped Tie allowed an elegant shrug. 'I'm perfectly sure that nobody else could. But Dolan can say he's Seyer's priest—'

'Prrriest!' Paul Frei had half risen, growling gutturally. He had once been a Catholic and was bitterly offended. 'Priest!'

'They could call him that in England,' Striped Tie said mildly.

'God in heaven—an untrained rascal.'

'I share your disapproval but I assure you that I'm also right.'

Paul Frei was recovering slowly. When he had himself in hand he said: 'There are two small points still. I shall be sending you a Brief for Dolan to work with. One of my men has been warned to prepare it. Most top scientists know what the others are doing, it is only the final breaks which they do not. Dolan does not speak scientists' language but I do not think that is necessarily fatal. As much of the Brief as possible can be phrased as simply "Yes" or "No".' Frei hesitated an instant for he wasn't an insensitive man. 'Is Seyer still blind?'

'I'm told he can tell if there's somebody in the room, but I doubt if his sight's important. Jacky could hardly show him a typed questionnaire without his wondering where he got it and what it meant. Even Seyer would be suspicious.'

'You are right of course, but there could be difficulties for a layman.'

'Then make sure your Brief takes care of them. Dolan may not be a scientist but he isn't unintelligent.'

'Can you speak for his memory?'

'I can speak for his power to outquote the devil.'

'That is good. I will send a man with the Brief for your hand tomorrow.'

'And your second point?' Striped Tie asked smoothly.

'There is a Negro called Peter Dinoba who was present at Seyer's accident.'

'I was wondering when you'd ask about him.'

'I am asking now. Do you think he killed Victor Lomax for the Executive?'

'No.'

'Nor do I. Do you think he killed Victor Lomax?'

'I don't know that. Do you want me to find out?'

'That is not yet necessary. But you will naturally keep a watch on him.'

'I already am. A close one.'

Dominy's report had been a difficult one for Laver.

He'd done right, Richard Laver thought, to have driven away without calling at Lomax's: there'd been two police cars and an ambulance and he couldn't have said that his presence was just coincidence. His face was well known to most police in London and simply to have appeared at all would have blown the Executive's interest in Lomax, something he'd rightly declined to do without permission from the Head of it. But he'd been making discreet inquiries since, not from the police which would have compromised him equally, but from sources which years of service had made available. The results had been simple but the inferences were scaring. Victor Lomax had been found strangled. There'd been a gun and it was his. Two shots had been fired but they'd found only one bullet.

So how would the police now handle it? Presumably as they normally did, by starting on Lomax's contacts. Unless it had been a professional job, and Laver's strong guess was it wasn't that, there'd be fingerprints all over the place but they wouldn't be a known criminal's. Then the police would fall back on the usual drill, a series of cosy chats at some station. Richard Laver smiled tolerantly. The prints wouldn't have been identified so the police would give you a paper to read or maybe offer a cigarette case. It wasn't against those iniquitous Judges' Rules.

And when they'd got prints which tallied, whose would they be? To Laver it looked a very fair bet. Three people had heard what Mervin Seyer had said—himself, Victor Lomax and Peter Dinoba. Lomax was dead and the Executive hadn't killed him. That left only Dinoba, who moreover had motive. More accurately he might think he had, and he *would* think he had if he'd ever mistrusted Lomax. It was clear that he had or he wouldn't have been in that car at all. There he had heard what Seyer had said about S.P.D. and black men, and Dinoba was both black himself and an intelligent, highly educated man. If he'd suspected that Lomax had private plans it would have been sensible to talk to him. What happened then was a guess on a guess. The talk went off the rails perhaps—it was the sort which could easily do so. All they knew was the gun was Lomax's. *He* must have pulled it.

Two questions, two probable answers. The third was more difficult since on its answer depended immediate action. Should the Executive pass to the police its guess, that of Lomax's various contacts Dinoba had powerful motive? Laver frowned for it was difficult. There was a tradition in the Executive which had weathered the years with honour: you never kept the police in the dark when an ordinary crime came across your path, and even with political crime you told them when there was mutual motive. But put Dinoba in a police cell now and you put the Executive's side of the case in blinkers. Laver hated to lose his only lead and with Dinoba in custody he'd be blinder than a bat.

He thought hard, then decided. Tell the police and you'd save them a day or two, some unfruitful inquiries of people with solid alibis, but equally hold your peace and you wouldn't ditch them. They'd find their own way to Dinoba in time though they'd probably find it cautiously. He had a respectable position and he happened to be coloured. The police had had some embarrassments with coloureds in recent weeks, so they wouldn't be taking a chance on him, they wouldn't be grilling a respectable black, far less arresting him, till they were perfectly sure it was open and shut. That could take three or four days and those days could be priceless.

Laver rang to Martin Dominy. 'One thing about this report of yours.'

'What's that?'

'The second bullet. If Dinoba's got a slug in him they'll pick him up when he goes to a doctor.'

'There are doctors of his own race who'd treat a gunshot wound without reporting it. It can't be a very serious one or he wouldn't have walked away with it.'

'Where is he now?'

'He's back in his flat.'

'Is he going to his office?'

'Not today. I rang it on an excuse and he hadn't come in.'

'You've got a man on him?'

'After this—of course.'

'Change him. Take it yourself. I know all about being a desk man now but it's a good thing to get away from it.'

'So I've noticed.'

Richard Laver rang off though he wasn't offended. Martin wouldn't have forgotten that he'd gone riding in Lightlove's cab himself.

He mixed himself a drink, a little easier but not much. The trouble with the Executive was that the harder you swam the further out the tide carried you. He had expected that, but not quite so bitter a struggle nor quite so soon . . . Paul von Frei. They had a fine fat file and a formidable man stared out from its pages, but Laver had never met him and now would have given much to do so. Was Martin Dominy's guess really right, that Frei wanted S.P.D. to exploit its antidote? Hm . . . Possible—not disprovable. Richard Laver frowned, for it wouldn't be how he'd have thought himself . . . Biological warfare. There'd been a Convention forty-odd years ago which had outlawed its use in any form, and though two major states had declined to sign there was now much talk of a new one. Richard Laver, a realist, was far from hopeful. The Powers could sign treaties all night if they wished and no sensible man slept a wink the sounder, not without mutual inspection, that is, and you didn't get that so easily. In practice you didn't get it at all unless public opinion forced its governments to concede it. On past form that was very unlikely indeed but it wasn't quite impossible. Richard Laver wasn't the only man who woke sweating in the small hours.

But suppose, just suppose, the talk ended in something effective, say mutual inspection and the bare grain of a mutual trust. Then no government would have S.P.D. but Paul Frei would . . . Money? No, Frei wasn't greatly interested now. But power remained. What sort of power? Richard Laver silently shook his head. Nothing so crude as simple blackmail, some hypothetical immunizer which might not exist. That wasn't how Frei operated, nor would he need to. He'd do business still but he'd do it for straight power. He had the means and he had the incentives. He had interests in German steel, Italian shipping; above all he bossed Continental, and Continental was second for heavy chemicals in the world. So sooner or later some Great Power would be desperate and Frei would approach it if it hadn't put its own feelers out first. He'd have S.P.D. to trade and by that time more; whatever appalling children-in-sin his own scientists had misbegotten on it. When he'd make his own terms. Not money now—he had more than he needed. But concessions, franchises, contracts on the grandest scale. Laver could think of at least two states which might play on those terms with their backs against the wall. . . . Huge areas to develop still. Factories, generators, irrigation schemes, power. A closed market to clinch it. Power. Industrial and commercial power on a scale no man had dared dream of.

Richard Laver shook his head again. Frei's long-term plans hardly mattered for the moment: Martin Dominy might be right and himself quite wrong. In either case what mattered now was simply Paul von Frei himself. He wasn't a man who gave up easily.

Which returned Richard Laver sharply to the matter of Peter Dinoba. Another attempt by Frei meant another plan, and Dinoba was a long loose end from an earlier plan which had broken down.

Paul Frei was a German, Germans hated loose ends.

10

Jacky D had met no one like Striped Tie in his life nor dreamed of such a sum as a hundred grand. Striped Tie had called in person since he could see no reason not to; if Jacky agreed then he would naturally keep his mouth shut and if he didn't agree the conversation could be repudiated. It was certain there wouldn't be witnesses. Striped Tie had had the flat watched discreetly, then, when he knew that Doris had gone shopping, had come himself quite openly, using his own name and his legitimate business card.

As he'd fully intended he'd shaken Jacky, not only by his proposal but by the manner of it, the casual candour. Jacky Dolan wasn't a worldly man but had sensed at once that this must be very big business indeed. Striped Tie had talked of his principal, apologizing with his lawyer's smile if the word sounded somewhat formal. Mr. Dolan would realize the difficulties.

Jacky started to ask questions and Striped Tie had answered them frankly. Frankly and so calmly it had been scaring. . . . Why had he come to Jacky when Mervin Seyer had older-established contacts?

A legitimate doubt which Striped Tie must remove: co-operation would be impossible if any shadow of mutual mistrust persisted. So there *had* been an earlier plan, another contact. His name had been Victor Lomax and he was dead. Striped Tie held a hand up coolly. No, one mustn't jump to absurd conclusions; he was as much in the dark about Lomax's death as no doubt was Mr. Dolan himself, but much better than any assurances were the simple facts of a business relationship. Victor Lomax had been his principal's man, who therefore hadn't a motive to lose him, far less to kill.

Jacky had thought this over: it sounded sense . . . So he

himself was a second best?

Say rather that he was a second choice, but that didn't mean that his chances were considered poor. On the contrary they'd always been thought to be good, so good they had been an embarrassment. Striped Tie, when he wished, could be decidedly engaging, and now he turned the charm on. His principal might be ruthless but he was also a very practical man, and so long as he'd been backing Lomax, Victor Lomax must be given a clear run. Which Mr. Dolan could have impeded if he'd got to Mervin Seyer first. To stop that directly would have been possible at a certain cost, that cost, to put it bluntly, being simply Mr. Dolan's life, but his principal hadn't wished for that so he'd tackled the problem differently. Not to stop Mr. Dolan getting the information but to make it very difficult to use it credibly if he did.

It took a minute for the penny to drop, then Jacky let his jaw fall. So that affair at his Rally *had* been organized to discredit him, the business at the B.B.C. to stop his mouth—cold-blooded and brutally, to cover a possible risk that old Seyer would say too much to him. Which was precisely what they were now suggesting, that he go to Mervin Seyer and pick his brains. For a hundred thousand pounds at that.

Jacky stared at Striped Tie dubiously: he let him stare. Striped Tie lived in a different world but he could guess how Jacky's mind would work. First the sense of outrage at the unembarrassed statement that his career had been broken wantonly, then astonishment and disbelief that a plan could be changed so drastically. Striped Tie would have liked to laugh but did not dare. It was certainly a *volte face*, really classic in its simplicity, typical of the tycoon's power to cut his first losses and start again. Paul Frei could surprise Striped Tie himself and he'd been working for him for several years. To this provincial little nonentity the mind of Paul Frei would be as strange as a man's from Mars.

Striped Tie let Jacky think, then gently nudged him. 'It's really extremely simple, you know.'

'It doesn't sound simple to me at all.'

'I don't see why not. Mervin Seyer is very dependent on you. Spiritually, if I may use the word. You could think of yourself as his father confessor.'

'I suppose I could.' Jacky D sounded doubtful.

'Rejoice. The position is worth a hundred thousand pounds. More precisely S.P.D. is.'

'And if I decline it?'

'I'm not here to threaten you.'

Jacky said uncertainly: 'Can I think it over?'

'I'm afraid there isn't too much time. We must know by two o'clock.' Striped Tie passed a card over, the small but respectable firm of City solicitors. As his cover it was invaluable. 'Ring me there, please—say "Yes" or "No". If "Yes" I will bring you a banker's draft for fifty thousand pounds as an advance.' His manner changed faintly but he was still most polite. 'I understand that the connection with your Committee has been ended.'

'Yes.'

'And that you do not wish to return to the mission field.'

'No, I do not.'

'Also that you have certain, er, calls on your private purse.'

Jacky Dolan didn't answer and Striped Tie rose. 'Thank you for receiving me. By two o'clock, then? Good.' He put a sealed envelope on the table. 'That is a Brief, though it is really only for guidance. Unsigned, of course. I needn't say that you cannot show it to Mervin Seyer. I think you well understand what we want.'

'You want everything about S.P.D. I understand that much, but I don't understand how I can talk to Mervin Seyer. He's in a hospital—'

'Nursing home.' Tie wrote the address down. 'Rather a

special nursing home but I won't weary you with that. You're his father confessor, they won't keep you out.'

'I'll have to think it over still.'

'Then I needn't take more of your time.'

Jacky Dolan sat down to think again. He'd been euphoric in his hospital, certain the break was coming. It hadn't come. On the contrary he'd frantically called off the *Gong*, frightened of something he hadn't known, terrified of uncertain consequences. But at least he wasn't uncertain now, he knew who'd been going after him, he knew the reason. Which clearly no longer existed—that weighed a lot. Now these same brutal people were bidding for his services, with a hundred thousand pounds and fifty down. He looked round the two-roomed flat, not quite squalid but deadly depressing. The rent was overdue and Doris was shopping. They had debts at the shops and their credit was shaky. He had two pounds in his pocket, maybe ten in the bank. The Committee's hundred and fifty had melted away. As for Anna Vescovi he hadn't seen her for a week.

Nevertheless he hesitated. Money—a hundred thousand pounds. It was almost too much. He'd never imagined a sum of that order and would simply have been suspicious if there hadn't been fifty thousand down. A banker's draft that afternoon and time to pay it in before they shut. Time to write Anna a cheque as well. The last one had bounced and she hadn't been pleased.

Still he couldn't decide. Not from conscience or not primarily (he'd have admitted he had that disciplined now) but from the knowledge that he was out of his league. Selective Pigmentation Disease. He had realized what that might mean and yet he hadn't. It was indecent, disgusting, horrible. Which were words of course, like good and bad, words till some man whom he'd never know sent a lawyer-type round with a hundred thou. So it was worth a hundred grand to some unknown man. What sort of man and where? What race? Jacky would never know that and he couldn't guess. In this world he'd be walking blind and he always would.

He was groping still, undecided, as Doris Dolan came in from her shopping. She didn't greet him or even offer a smile but took the shopping bag into the kitchen. For something to do he followed her, watching her unpack the bag. There were cold ham and pickles and sliced bread wrapped in cellophane. He loathed the stuff, it choked him and made him constipated. She caught his look and said in the ladylike voice he'd grown to hate:

'If you want to eat better I'll have to have more money. We owe at the shops again.'

'I've twelve pounds in the world.'

'Then you'd better get a job.'

'What job?'

'The civil service wants clerks.'

'What makes you think they'd take me?'

'You need only read and write.' She looked at him. 'And they don't make too many inquiries just for clerks.'

For the first time and last he hit her.

The result was sensational, the second of an astonishing morning. She sat down and laughed, not her tee-hee lady's giggle but something dangerously near a snarl. It wasn't an agreeable sound. 'Thank you for that,' she said. 'That lets me out.'

He started to say: 'I'm sorry,' but she silenced him impertinently.

'I'm not. Now listen Jacky D that was. I'm your wife and I mean to stay that way. You follow me?'

'No, I don't.' But he did.

'I know all about that woman of yours. I know her name and I know where she lives.' She couldn't resist the banal comment. 'I'm sorry for her with a man like you.'

'She's sorry for *you*,' Jacky D said simply.

'How dare she! Not that it matters what prostitutes think. You can go to her—I can't stop you. But I'll never divorce you. Never.'

He went back into the living-room, walking to the wall cupboard, tugging at the ill-fitting door. Inside was the last of Lomax's whisky and Jacky D poured and drank it.

The telephone rang and he went to it.

At first it was a jumble of words, something about a nursing home. The woman speaking was urgent but she wasn't very lucid. Jacky interrupted her.

'I follow that you're a nursing home. Who's speaking?'

'I'm the matron.'

'And that somebody wants to talk to me.'

'Mervin Seyer—he's asking for you. I don't think he's going to last much longer. He says he's got to see you before he goes.'

He looked at the clock; it was half past eleven. He hadn't time now to think or fear and secretly was glad he hadn't. By two o'clock, the man had said . . .

'I'm starting now.'

In the taxi he opened the Brief and read it. He would have liked more than the twenty minutes in a taxi from north London but he knew that he'd never have them now. When things happened at this pace you went with the stream. You went with it or not at all.

Only a bare week ago Peter Dinoba would have known what to do without hesitation. He'd have gone straight to the police as a matter of course and he'd have told them the whole story, that he'd heard old Mervin Seyer talk and that it had frightened him severely. Another man had been present, one whose motives he'd distrusted, so he'd gone round to talk it out with him and this man had pulled a gun and threatened. There'd been a struggle and Peter had strangled him, though he hadn't intended a killing. There was a bullet in the room which the police could trace and another in Peter Dinoba too, so they'd find it all as he said it was. But now he was thinking differently, not with his brain but instinctively, with his viscera. Victor Lomax had been white and Peter wasn't; the police were white also and so was England. Peter was too intelligent to suppose that they wouldn't pick him up, but it simply wasn't thinkable to walk voluntarily into this white man's net. Let them find him when they could and do their worst. He hadn't by now the smallest doubt that they'd fix him given the slightest chance.

Of course they would—they'd be bound to. All men were enemies, white men especially. In the fog of his fear and uncertainty Peter was lonely as never before, so he'd have to talk to somebody and only one man knew the background as he did. Or rather it was a woman. If he went to Margaret Seyer then at least he needn't explain from scratch; she knew all about Lomax, she'd mistrusted him too. She might not understand it all but at least they had knowledge in common. He could face Margaret Seyer but not explanations.

Nevertheless he had gone to her with some diffidence, uncertain of his reception. He knew she was in London now in a flat which a friend had lent her, but she had troubles of her own and plenty; Margaret was watching her father die. She might not want to see him and on the telephone she'd been reserved and cool, but she'd have half an hour after lunch that day, and if it was really as urgent as Peter said she'd be pleased to see him.

She let him in quietly, not hostile but not welcoming either; she looked at his arm in a sling and asked at once:

'What have you done to your arm?'

'I hurt it,' he said dismissively. He had considered a much

more detailed story, some tale about a domestic mishap, but he hated lies and he knew he lied unconvincingly. 'It's nothing,' he added.

She looked at the sling. 'Have you been to a doctor?'

'Yes, of course.'

It was true enough though he wished to forget it. The experience had shaken him, the shabby practice in south London, the squalid and unswept waiting room, the quarrelling children. Nevertheless he had chosen deliberately. The doctor was one of his own new nation though not of Peter Dinoba's clan. That was the point. He was going to treat a gunshot wound, more precisely to take a bullet out, and he'd know he'd have a duty to report it to the police. Equally Peter knew he wouldn't. He was a Coast man, recently qualified, and he'd know at once what Peter stood for; he'd have kinsmen in the country still and he wouldn't dare put them at risk from what he feared. Which was the Peter Dinobas, all of them. So he'd taken the two-two slug from the forearm a little clumsily. He had given Peter a local but he hadn't pretended it still wouldn't hurt. As it had. Peter had set his teeth and borne it. The doctor had urged a hospital but Peter wouldn't hear of it. Once in hospital they'd put him out and once he was out he'd be sitting game.

Margaret was asking coolly: 'Nothing broken?'

'No, just a flesh wound.'

She opened her mouth but shut it again. Men, black or white, were quite absurd. He'd probably been boiling a kettle and let it slip. A scald, one caught cooking. He'd be insanely ashamed of that so he'd cover up. 'You sounded worried on the phone,' she said.

'I am.'

'Better tell me.' She looked at her watch as she spoke but she said it.

He'd had time to think things over, to compress what was

inessential. 'I got into Lomax's car with your father—'

'I know what happened, my cousin told me. He sent my father to a nursing home and he had to tell me the why of it.'

'So that man who arrived was your cousin from the Executive?'

'I gave you his number but I guessed you wouldn't use it. I thought he ought to know so I rang him myself.'

She wasn't defensive but matter-of-fact and Peter Dinoba in no way blamed her. He'd thought once before it was proper to use one's family. Even whites sometimes trusted their kinsmen, and the man at risk from Lomax had been her father. But he looked at her uncertainly for she was suddenly a stranger. He hated to face the word and chose another. Say rather she wasn't the woman he'd known. This wasn't the Margaret Seyer whose rose . . .

'If you know what happened you'll know it all. You'll know your father thought Lomax was Jacky D. He started to talk about S.P.D.—'

'Yes, I do know that.' She sounded impatient. 'Now Lomax is dead—I've seen the papers.' The clear blue eyes under the formidable eyebrows sharpened. 'And I could guess what you might be thinking too, that Richard Laver had Lomax put quietly away. You'd be wrong as hell if you thought like that, that isn't my cousin's form at all.'

'No,' he said simply, 'I never thought that.'

'You might have, it's perfectly logical.'

'No, not logical in the least.'

'Which can only mean that you've guessed who did it.'

'Yes,' he said, 'I think I have.'

He had expected to be questioned and was ready to let her judge him. But no questions came. He saw the blue eyes slide down to his sling, then they slid away as casually. She said finally, indifferently:

'I'm not interested in Lomax now, he seems to have got

what he asked for. I'm interested in my father and the doctors don't hold much hope for him.'

'I needn't tell you how sorry I am.' It sounded pathetically stilted and formal.

She flared at him unexpectedly. 'You needn't but you ought to, you and all that damned Committee. If my father hadn't got hooked in that net none of this would have happened. No Lomax, no Jacky D—'

'I came here to talk about Jacky D.'

'What about him?'

'Your father wanted to talk to him. If he managed to talk still—'

'Oh God,' she said, 'oh God, oh God.' She was angry now but not with Peter, for she had caught herself thinking as she'd never believed she'd dare to think. They were all the same, these men of colour, Indians, Arabs, Negroes, the lot. They cut themselves into games with whites and when they lost money they screamed they'd been cheated. They played with the nursery fire and burnt their fingers, then off they went yelping to big white nanny. She suppressed the thought contemptuously though she didn't quite expunge it, but she managed to say in her normal voice:

'Listen, Peter. Please listen carefully. I'm bitter about all this, I'm bitter as hell. My father would never have climbed right back but he wouldn't have been dying if he hadn't got in with Jacky and all the rest of you. I don't say you're responsible, Pete, but I do say you're connected.' She summoned the ghost of her usual smile. 'I'm sorry but that's how I feel just now. And I never felt like you did about Jacky.'

'I don't really know how I feel about Jacky myself. Not any more. But your father wanted to talk to him—'

'And you're frightened of that?'

'Very frightened indeed.'

'If you're thinking about that S.P.D.—'

'I am.'

'So am I, but as a daughter. S.P.D.'s on my father's conscience. I'd bless the man who could ease him, even Jacky.' She looked at him again, not angry still but worse, impersonal. 'I don't think you quite trust Jacky now.'

He spread his lean hands. 'You ask difficult questions.'

The black eyebrows came down in thought once more though she'd half decided. She said at last:

'I like you, Peter, I'd like to play fair. Jacky D saw my father this morning.'

He stood up at once. 'How do you know?'

'The nursing home rang me just before lunch.'

'What did your father tell him?'

'I don't know that—I can guess it, though. Father's sleeping peacefully, the first time without sedatives since the accident.' She looked at her watch again. 'I'm going to see him in half an hour.'

He said miserably, forcing the words out: 'Conscience . . . Jacky . . . Peacefully sleeping.'

She put a hand out but drew it back again. That wouldn't help now, might make it worse. 'I thought I owed it to you to tell you.'

'You owed it to my race,' he said. He'd never spoken about his race before, nor thought it, to Margaret Seyer, worth a mention.

He went back to his flat in a cruising taxi and Martin Dominy tailed it smoothly. He was out on a job, enjoying it, but any trained man would have noticed what he had. There was a second car tailing Peter Dinoba and it was doing it very skilfully.

Jacky went up the steps of the nursing home, seeing it was an expensive one. The hall was painted white, there were many fresh flowers in elaborate vases, and in a cubicle a doorman who rose as Jacky came in. He looked the standard Commissionaire, the ex-soldier, the good old sweat.

'Can I help you, sir?'

'I've come to see Mr. Seyer.'

'Have you an appointment, sir?'

'I certainly have. The matron phoned me.'

'Did she indeed?' There was something about the man's manner which Jacky thought odd. He was polite enough but he wasn't obliging. 'I'll ring the Duty Doctor, sir.'

Jacky D couldn't hear what the doctor said but he heard the Commissionaire clearly.

'I'm afraid the doctor says it's out of the question.'

'But the matron rang me.'

'I'm sorry, sir.'

Jacky wasn't taking it, not from this officious old sergeant. There was a board on the wall and he looked at it . . . Mervin Seyer, Number Twenty-four. That would probably be on the second floor. Jacky started towards the stairs and the sergeant said politely:

'I wouldn't do that, sir, if I was you.'

'Oh, be quiet.'

The sergeant sighed but he knew his drill. He pressed a red button firmly.

Jacky ran up the stairs to the right-angled turn, changing stride on the landing to hold the bend. The split second saved him from the worst of it since the timing was set for a normal walk. Nevertheless he bought the lot. He never saw clearly what happened or how but he knew he fell down and he fell very hard.

When he came to he was lying on a clinical bed. Two white-coated doctors were talking quietly in a corner. He could hear them but only just.

'He doesn't look like a strongarm.'

'Not a bit. And there's no weapon.'

'Just impulsive.'

'Very.' The older doctor frowned. 'Did the doorman check his story about the matron having rung him?'

'Not after what you said to him.'

'It would be interesting to talk to her just the same.' He picked up a telephone and Jacky again heard a woman's voice. When she had finished the doctor put the receiver down. 'Very awkward indeed.' He was clearly undecided and walked back thoughtfully to Jacky's cot. 'Ah,' he said professionally. 'Conscious again. That's good.'

'What happened?'

'You were running upstairs and you're a little too old for it. You fell down and you hit the banister. There's a bump on your forehead—'

'I thought something hit me.' He could remember very little, he was confused and the doctor saw it.

'Whatever could? Just be careful with strange stairs, though.' The doctor rubbed his chin as he thought. 'Are you Mr. James Dolan?' he asked at length.

Jacky D nodded. It hurt his head.

'I hope I don't sound too rude if I ask you to establish it.'

'There's a driving licence in my pocket-book.'

The doctor went to a coat on a hanger. 'Yes . . . And you're a priest?'

'I'm not ordained.'

The doctor's smile was quick and cool. 'Let's say a man of religion, then.'

'I'm that.'

'You know Mr. Seyer well?'

'He sent for me,' Jacky D said simply.

'Alas, he did.' The older doctor had been hesitating but now he had made his mind up. Turning to the younger he said: 'We'll give him ten minutes more rest, then we'll take him up.'

'You mean it?'

'We must.'

The doctors smiled briefly and went away. Jacky heard the key turn.

They went into another room, a surprising room for a nursing home. One wall was a bank of switches and dials, sophisticated and formidable electronics. The younger man said uneasily:

'I know someone who won't approve what we're doing.'

'So do I but he'll have to take it.'

'Suppose he doesn't see it like that and we'll be standing against a blank white wall.'

'Use your head as our mutual friends will. There are things we can do here and things we can't. One of them's keeping a priest from a dying man. I know he isn't a proper priest but he's the man Mervin Seyer sent for. If a newspaper got hold of that—'

The younger man said in audible headlines: ' "Doctor Refuses Last Rites to Patient." '

'Don't frighten me more than I'm scared already. We have to do what we're doing but we can still insure the result a bit. You put him in a bugged room of course?'

'Of course.'

The first doctor went to the wall panel, pressing the switch marked '24'. He turned another on the recorder below and the tape began to run on it. The doctor looked at his watch.

'Ten minutes—we'll take him up.'

'I hope we're doing right, my God I do.'

11

Richard Laver had been summoned for a discussion with Mr. Lloyd Milligan. Summoned, he reflected, as he walked briskly up Whitehall, was the wrong word constitutionally, but Milligan wasn't a tactful man and some of his private arrogance had rubbed off on to his staff. The secretary who had telephoned had been brusque to the point of rudeness. Laver had considered him ill-mannered but not worse, knowing that Private Secretaries took their mores from their masters. Let them do so if they wished to since the position was unchanged by it. Which in fact was that two Ministers could give instructions to Richard Laver, and only two. They were the Prime Minister and his own, and he knew that Charles Russell had both respected Tuke and liked him. Harry Tuke you could do business with. Serve Harry Tuke loyally, as Russell had, and he'd look after you in the pinches; he certainly wouldn't tolerate that Lloyd Milligan break the protocol.

Laver knew he had not done so since he'd telephoned on the private line. . . . He, Harry Tuke, was in something of an embarrassment. They probably shared an opinion of one of Tuke's Cabinet colleagues, but the fact remained that his Department was formally responsible for what went on at that place in Wiltshire. So Tuke had shown him Laver's latest report since not to have done so would clearly have been unfriendly. And the damned man had asked to discuss it directly. It would serve no known purpose but to avoid offending Milligan, but that was still worth doing. Just. Then if Laver would oblige . . .? He would? That was really extremely kind of him. And afterwards Tuke would buy him lunch since it was certain that Milligan wouldn't.

So Laver sat down in Lloyd Milligan's room, prepared to be just as courteous as Lloyd Milligan was polite to him.

He feared that the standard might not be high. The Minister tapped the report on his desk, saying in his high Hampstead squeak:

'Disastrous.'

'Perhaps.'

'Don't you agree?'

'I don't dissent, Minister.'

'Let us take your report, then. What Mervin Seyer blurted out was the *nature* of a secret, not its details. In the light of past events that's potentially very dangerous, but the damage can be contained if the people who heard him blurt can be contained. Or so you seem to feel.'

He's enjoying this, Richard Laver thought; he's showing off his first class brain. Laver said simply: 'Yes.'

'So five men were concerned and I propose to take them singly. First yourself, who of course are secure.' The Minister made an unnecessary bow. When he wasn't being arrogant he was tiresomely ingratiating. 'Then the driver of your car—'

'Who did not come near us till after Seyer had lost consciousness.'

'Oh . . . I see.' It had been in the report but Lloyd Milligan had missed it. Conscious that he'd dropped a point he reacted in irritation. 'But Mervin Seyer,' he said sharply.

'Is now safely in a nursing home.'

'When you say "safely"—'

'I am speaking from private knowledge. This nursing home isn't a prison, nor has anyone any legal right to keep Seyer there if he wishes to leave. But I'm quite sure he won't. He's a very sick man and quite possibly dying. We have very good connections with the nursing home in question.'

'Accepting that he won't leave it, could the Press get in to see him?'

'Almost certainly not, but that's formally for the doctors.'

'With whom you have connections, I think you said.'

'Close connections.'

'I don't like it at all,' the Minister said, and Richard Laver suppressed a thoughtful sigh. He knew now why Harry Tuke held one of the five great Offices of State and he knew why Lloyd Milligan would never succeed in doing so. His background was academic, middle class, but there'd been others in his party who'd surmounted these shameful obstacles. Lloyd Milligan's private ball and chain was something more fundamental; he was a smart little intellectual who believed himself intelligent. He was saying now fretfully:

'Then take the remaining two, the African and Lomax. Both were connected with Seyer through their interest in this Jacky D. What do you know against Jacky D?'

'Put like that—nothing. He went on telly on Thursday where he swore and blew his career apart.'

'But according to this report of yours you believe he was going to say something. If that's right, where did he get it?'

'From Seyer, I think—we can't escape that. But that's water over the dam by now.'

'I don't like it,' Lloyd Milligan said again; he froze in a pose of self-conscious thought. 'But when Seyer himself went much further than the name there were two men present besides yourself. They were this African and Lomax. Both had explicable contacts with Mervin Seyer. What about Victor Lomax, deceased? As I understand it, you were present because of Lomax.'

Laver said deliberately: 'We had been given information that Lomax's relationship with Seyer might not be wholly innocent.' He was very seldom pompous.

'Surely that's understating it.' The Minister waved the report a little crossly. His temper, never predictable, was fraying. Laver noticed it indifferently. He wasn't playing the interview to irritate a Minister, but he wasn't a man to decline an advantage. His private opinion of Lloyd Milligan was that the Minister was a clever fool, and clever fools who lost their tempers were easy meat.

'According to this report I have Lomax was driving in a way to invite an accident.'

'He got one at that. Not quite what he'd planned, though.' Laver realized at once that the words had two meanings. He hadn't intended a *double entendre* but it hadn't escaped the Minister. Lloyd Milligan was looking at him, and if he hadn't been a Minister his expression would have been simply sly. 'Ah,' he said, 'I see.'

. . . The bloody man thinks we murdered Lomax.

'Then coming to this African—'

'A Christian who lost his faith and recovered it from Jacky D. Hence the contact. Degree from your own university. His country struck diamonds and licensed them to de Masseys. He's Number Two at the London end.'

'Background?'

Laver hesitated. Dominy's private shorthand for Dinoba had been upper class black, and Laver had accepted the phrase since he knew very well what Dominy meant. But he doubted that Lloyd Milligan would, he'd probably bridle, might even attempt a ponderous snub. Laver said telegraphically:

'Northerner. Feudal. Family. Land.'

'He doesn't sound attractive.'

'But he is.'

The Minister reluctantly let it pass. He would have liked to read Richard Laver a lesson but he guessed that he couldn't annoy him. Laver would simply listen politely, then return to the matter of Peter Dinoba. The Minister fought his temptation and won. It wasn't his business to teach what he thought unteachable. He said instead:

'Poor Seyer mentioned black men and Peter Dinoba's an African. What has he done since the accident?'

'No newspaper has had anything about what happened on the motorway, which means that he hasn't been to one. There's been no diplomatic rumpus, which there would have been if he'd gone to his High Commissioner.'

'But he could still be considering his position, taking advice?'

'He could.'

The Minister's manner became the schoolmaster's he'd been, patient, infuriating without knowing it. 'Then who do you think is behind all this?'

'An old client of ours whom we've tangled with before.'

'You're not going to tell me his name?'

'Since I'm guessing without a shadow of proof I don't think I ought to risk a slander.' Laver was bland as the bishop he detested.

Lloyd Milligan was furious but Lloyd Milligan had to take it. He knew the position perfectly. Richard Laver was present by courtesy of Harry Tuke and Milligan hated Harry Tuke as the little man loathes the big one. This damned superior policeman would walk straightaway to Harry Tuke, and he'd give him the name at once if Tuke happened to ask it; then they'd relax over drinks and a friendly chat, this courteous well-spoken killer and that stupid Trades Union hack with the political luck he himself didn't have. He couldn't admit it was other than luck.

The last of his temper flew ungracefully out of the window as he said dangerously: 'We're concerned with a state secret. What are you going to do about it?'

'About Dinoba? We'll have to look at that.'

The Minister exploded. 'It simply isn't good enough. My Department is involved.'

'Then may I ask what you suggest?'

'Fix him, of course,' Lloyd Milligan snarled. 'It wouldn't be the first time from what you say.'

Richard Laver was quietly furious but he didn't let Milligan see it. What would happen if he blacked the man's eye, then went straight to the *Gong* with the story? Even the *Gong* wouldn't print it cold, but if the Head of the Executive happened to lose his job shortly after . . .

It was a pipe dream though mildly tempting. Richard Laver got his temper back for he'd seen this before and he didn't like it. It was strange, he was thinking, the intellectuals' love of a violence they couldn't achieve and wouldn't dare. The cult of the intellectual armed. Very odd, very interesting. One day he'd write a paper on it. For the moment he said placidly:

'You want Dinoba arrested?'

'If that will be sufficient.'

'Will you give me a warrant?' It was the first time he'd been naughty, far less consciously provocative, and it stopped Lloyd Milligan dead in his tracks. He said soberly:

'You know I can't do that.'

'Yet you were asking me to fix him.'

'Well . . .' The Minister was defensive, more than a little scared that he'd be quoted.

'The point is not that but a different one. If we'd done as you think we'd have done it on our own judgment. We don't run a shop with lives for sale, not even with Tuke as customer.'

'Harry Tuke!' The Minister was more than defensive now—Laver could see he was bitterly offended. He didn't much care since the interview was over.

'With whom I'm having lunch in half an hour.' Richard Laver rose and found his hat. 'Good morning, Minister.'

As he walked to Pall Mall and to Harry Tuke's club Laver

was smiling gently, but not with malice nor even with pleasure. It gave him no lift to have infuriated Milligan, for he hadn't tried to best him, had indeed held his punches till obliged to defend himself. He was genuinely amused. Why, a junior civil servant could have handled the interview better. A few simple and courteous questions would have brought simple and courteous answers, for instance that Richard Laver was a civilized and a decent man. He detested the thought of S.P.D. and would be delighted not to have heard of it.

He never made luncheon at Harry Tuke's club. Martin Dominy was on the steps of it and a faceless black saloon in the street below. Dominy said simply: 'Come.'

'I'll have to leave a message.'

'Hurry.'

In the Executive Dominy turned on the tape. Laver ran it three times, then sent for the senior boffin. What had impressed him was that he could understand much of it. The second class scientist loved his jargon as he loved his life since he lacked the simple disciplines to use simple words effectively, but Seyer had been a teacher too and Laver had heard that he'd rated high. Now, if he'd ever doubted, his doubts had gone. Seyer had spoken untechnically, the master of quiet exegesis. He had answered some questions "Yes" or "No", but when that hadn't been possible, he'd been as lucid as a midnight bell. Laver wasn't a scientist but he was experienced at grading them. This one was unmistakably first class.

When the boffin arrived Richard Laver explained in six grim sentences. The boffin let his breath out.

'It's not my line but I'll get it evaluated. I know just the man.'

'Is he secure?'

'She is.'

'As soon as possible, please.'

Laver settled to think, a little frightened and not ashamed of it. He had known that in crisis the Executive stretched its Head to his human limits, but he'd accepted the job under no sort of pressure and he wasn't a man to complain of his own decisions. He even contrived a quick wry smile, partly at Richard Laver who'd bought it, but mostly at Lloyd Milligan who'd been scared as hell he'd be holding the baby. Which now they all too clearly were.

What drivel the man had talked, what pompous rot! 'State secret' indeed—S.P.D. wasn't that, or rather it wasn't some orthodox secret, something whose formal security Laver could pass to another and less delicate organization. S.P.D. was political, inescapably entangled with any government which had allowed its birth. It wasn't as though it were something straightforward, some new and non-nuclear explosive, say, which any Minister worth his salt could defend and would. Even if it had been nuclear there were plenty of people so tired of being spied on that they'd accept without too much fuss and noise any sensible action to stop the spying. But biological warfare was different in kind; it was a horrible thing and still horrifying publicly.

Which made talk of arrests and warrants merely futile. Jacky Dolan was now in clear breach of the law and could be arrested that day quite legally, but thereafter he'd have to be brought to trial, which could easily bring the house down. Few Ministers' heads would be safe on their shoulders.

Richard Laver tried to think like one, not like Lloyd Milligan who'd been shaken and jumpy, but like Harry Tuke or the Prime Minister. They'd got stuck with a strain of an old disease which would take on a black man and not a white. And how did you defend such a thing to a raging and outraged public opinion? You had a case of a sort, you might tell the truth, insisting you couldn't stop science (you hadn't tried), piously swearing you'd never use it, hinting, perfectly truly again, that the discovery wasn't your own alone. The last, Laver knew, was almost certainly the fact. Mervin Seyer had been to Fort Detrick often, so one's friends had it too and very possibly one's enemies, and even if they hadn't yet it would be a matter of months not years before they had. . . . Then all we had, dear friends and voters, was a piece of new science which other governments had too. Didn't you want your country to keep its seat at the Top Table?

Laver shook his head for it wouldn't do. Put that around in time where it mattered and you might just conceivably live with it, but it wouldn't be an answer if the Press had the story in headlines. Nor would it just be massed police in the streets when the banners went bloodily marching. Millions of ordinary citizens would be demanding to know the reason why.

And that wasn't the end by any means. You'd allowed such a thing to be born which was vile, but suppose it were known that you'd let it slip. Not to another government, where even the most unfriendly had established rules and a certain responsibility. No, to a single man. Paul Frei, a German. If that happened and the news seeped out then Lloyd Milligan's terror would look like a modest night sweat.

. . . Paul Frei who lived in Amsterdam. An hour's flight away and Laver had better be ready for it. He managed another uncertain smile. The Head of the Executive had one thing in common with royalty and only one: he couldn't leave the country without a Minister's permission.

He rang to Harry Tuke and got it.

12

What Jacky now thought an accident but was later to decide
was not had delayed him by half an hour at least, and it was a
quarter to two when at last he left Welbeck Street. He ran to
the nearest telephone booth and at once was on to Striped
Tie in person. He didn't sound much surprised or pleased but
said simply that he'd come round at once, and when Jacky
got back to his flat in a lather Striped Tie was waiting without impatience. So was a banker's draft for fifty thousand.

Jacky was pleased to see it, not only because he had still
time to cash it, but because the fact that Striped Tie had kept
his word was the first event in a hectic day which he'd come
anywhere near foreseeing. His talk with Mervin Seyer had
been easier than he'd expected. At first the old man had been
full of his sins, more anxious to talk of his wickedness than
of the brutal facts which made him wicked. But Jacky had
said that that was useless. Peace would come only from total
release, the terrible details, all of them. The Brief had been
helpful, but even without it Jacky D would have been
loaded. The story had come tumbling out, everything up to
the final tests, clearly and simply, happily, the fine brain
clearing as it ran strongly in familiar fields. Jacky wasn't a
scientist but now he almost believed he was. He'd even got
down a figure or two.

Jacky hadn't expected that and he'd expected still less what
Striped Tie now did; he hadn't had time to think in detail
but had supposed that Striped Tie would at least want the
outlines. Indeed he had started to talk of them but Striped
Tie had promptly silenced him: he didn't want Jacky's news
and far less his notes. Moreover he had explained why not.
The world he worked in didn't operate like that . . . Mr.
Dolan now had the essence or at least a most valuable lead
to it? Good. Then supposing he passed it to a man who was

merely an agent, where would the agent's principal stand? Striped Tie had answered the question, smiling. The principal would be at the agent's mercy, open to blackmail, the limitless squeeze. And that apart there was the technical aspect. Striped Tie was no scientist, nor was his principal, but his principal had them at convenient call. Naturally he'd wish to weigh before parting with further money for unseen goods. The first fifty thousand was safe, was indeed, Striped Tie saw, in Jacky's pocket, and there was still time to clear it before the bankers put their shutters up. As for the rest it would have to be earned. Jacky must go in person to Striped Tie's principal.

Jacky hadn't liked it and he held more than he'd dreamt in his pocket now, but Striped Tie had unerringly read his thought. He said politely but very firmly:

'I told you there was still time to clear that draft. There is also time to stop it.'

'Then to whom am I to go? And where? And when?'

'The "to whom" doesn't matter—that will all be taken care of. But the place is Amsterdam and the time must be this evening. There's a flight at seventeen twenty-five.'

'It's very short notice.'

'It's very big money.'

Jacky D thought it over. He was a reasonable man and he could see Striped Tie's viewpoint, but what he couldn't read was Striped Tie's mind. Who hadn't reached an eminence where men like Paul Frei employed him without a great deal of experience. He had expected that Jacky, a priest of a sort if the word must be prostituted, would be admitted to talk to Mervin Seyer, but he knew about that nursing home and was certain that the Executive would have heard about the visit. Probably Seyer's room had been bugged, which meant there'd be a tape of the whole talk. The Executive might not have grasped every word but they'd have scientists at call who would, and once the scientists had advised him Richard Laver would know where he stood at once. He would know with some relief for the position, if not his action, would now be certain. The action might well be a difficult choice, but Jacky had made a note or two, and these, with what he held in his head, were in breach of a potent and hard-toothed Act. Did he realize it yet? It hardly mattered. What was important was to get him out quickly.

He was saying now uncertainly: 'I'm not sure I can make the arrangements in time.'

'You mustn't worry about the arrangements—they've all been made. You will be met in Amsterdam of course, and a car will be calling for you at four. The driver will have your ticket.'

'I could go the Air Terminal.'

'You could,' Striped Tie said, 'but it's convenient to send for you.' He was thinking that 'convenient' was the understatement of a lifetime. The car would have two of his men in it and he wouldn't feel really happy till he had Jacky under their watchful wing. He would have liked to send the car at once, but Jacky would want to clear his draft, the paper was burning a hole in his pocket. To confront him prematurely with what were patently guards would be very bad organization indeed. It might start him thinking politically, of his own position and possible danger. Two hours of unaccustomed action had apparently inhibited that, but once he started to think he might not go. That would mean complications and complications were always deplorable.

Striped Tie took his leave and Jacky Dolan a taxi. He hadn't the money to pay for it but if he reached the bank in time he would. He would indeed.

At the bank he paid the draft in, writing a cheque for the

rent, one or two others for pressing bills. He transferred five hundred to Anna Vescovi, drawing two hundred more for immediate use. He had carried two hundred pounds before but they'd never been his own good pounds.

Back in the flat he had started to pack and Doris, returning, had interrupted. She had looked at the packing and sniffed disapprovingly. She was expert at sniffing.

'Sneaking off?' she had asked.

'You could call it that. *You* would.'

'I'm your wife.'

'So you told me.'

'You think you've got a job at last?'

'Perhaps.'

'I must know where.'

'Amsterdam,' he said. He hadn't been told he mustn't for Striped Tie hadn't thought that sensible. The least hint of a foolish secrecy and Jacky might take fright at once. Besides, he could be easily traced. As far as Amsterdam and then no further.

'Someone in Holland has offered you a job?' She was incredulous and sounded it.

'Mind your own bloody business.' He meant it very literally. Doris was on her own from now. She could always go back to Africa.

He was lying on his bed again, shaven now but in greater distress than ever. He could have borne a single emotion with the stoicism which his people admired and in childhood had taught him was virtue, but three swept him now unremittingly, like the waves of a well-planned attack in war, first the planes, then the armour, then the infantry to mop up. Hate first, then the sense of loss, then the desperate uncertainty.

The hate he could take, for unknowingly he'd been prepared for it. He wasn't a Christian now so hate was lawful. Once he'd been told he must love his enemies but that had been ridiculous: a man who couldn't hate was no man at all. So he'd killed Victor Lomax and that was that. He hadn't planned to take his life but if he'd known what he'd now found out he could well have done so. Victor Lomax had deserved his death since he'd been working to get S.P.D., to sell it to some unknown man whose name he hadn't uttered before he died. But a white, of course—no other had motive. For more years than he could remember Peter had thought of his colour seldom, but now that he must he wasn't ashamed. Why should he be ashamed? He could hate his enemies.

So he let the hate wash over him and the wounds it inflicted were not too severe, but then came the searing sense of loss and he had little defence against that or none. The attack was too insidious, the damage too sharp and personal . . . Margaret Seyer who'd slipped out of his life, angry a little and quite uncaring. She hadn't cared tuppence for S.P.D., it had been something her father had wished to confess and blessed the man who could lift his load. Later no doubt she would stop and think but later would never restore their relationship. He had gone to her for advice and help and at first she'd been angry, then calm, even friendly . . . 'I like you, Peter.' She'd liked him but she'd dismissed him empty.

He eased his arm in the sling which held it. At first it hadn't hurt him much but now he'd begun to wonder if that doctor had known his business. If he hadn't it could be awkward.

Peter didn't much care, this was physical pain, but the third wave of emotion was coming in now, the men with cold steel, the sharp uncertainty. If Seyer had talked to Jacky as priest he'd have told the whole story or none at all, when Jacky would know about S.P.D., the horror which Lomax had died without reaching. So what would he do with it, how would his mind work? He wasn't a wicked man, not of purpose like Victor Lomax, but Peter had worked in this white man's world and it had left him with few illusions. Jacky was discredited now, a man without a future, even a job. Put at its lowest he'd be vulnerable to temptation. Inevitably it would present itself and Jacky wasn't a saint but a penniless flop.

Peter climbed down from the bed with care, for even in minutes his arm had stiffened. He was smiling grimly. He didn't laugh loud or easily for he'd been taught it was undignified, but his clan had a taste for irony and this struck him as ironical. He'd have to talk to Jacky D, so twice in two days he'd be talking to white men of S.P.D. without a clear plan, simply probing at their intentions. It had worked the first time, though not as expected, for Lomax had pulled a gun on him. Well, he wouldn't kill Jacky, that much was sure. Jacky would never possess a gun and without a gun that would make it murder.

At the Dolans' flat Doris opened the door to him. She stared for a second, red-eyed and frowzy. Peter saw she had been crying.

'I'd like to talk to Jacky, please.'

'He's out.' She pulled the door wider, talking about a cup of tea. She'd always rather fancied Peter, though the thought, if she'd faced it, would have frozen her in abject shame. Not because he was black—he was also handsome. But she was a married woman and that was final.

'Is he coming back soon?'

'I really don't know.'

There was an uncertainty in her manner which conveyed

itself immediately. Normally she was acidulous but she wasn't usually frightened. Peter asked sharply:

'Where's he gone?'

'To Amsterdam.'

'What for?'

'He didn't tell me.'

She began to cry again messily, seeking his sympathy. 'Two men came round in a big black car. Only a couple of minutes ago. I saw one of them give him an air ticket.'

'What sort of men?'

'They looked pretty rough types.'

'Goodbye,' Peter said. 'Good luck to you.'

He left her protesting noisily and went home in the cab he'd kept waiting in case he needed it. . . . Amsterdam—that was easy. De Masseys had an office in Amsterdam. But why Amsterdam for Jacky who hadn't? It was futile to guess, he'd have to go and find out. He hadn't a doubt of that, he must go at once. Before Jacky did something final with S.P.D.

He looked at his watch as he paid off the taxi. It was half past four. He knew the flight times by heart since he visited Amsterdam at least once a month. The next was at seventeen twenty-five and there wasn't the time to go first to the Terminal. His arm was hurting him badly too and he couldn't have faced a ride in the crowded coach. He rang to his London office, quite sure of himself, the Number Two and aware of it . . . Something unexpected had cropped up in Amsterdam and he'd have to go over immediately. Ring at once for a place on the afternoon plane. He could make it with luck for take-off but he'd be late on the check-in time. The office would take care of that? Then send a car round at once, please. Yes, at once. An experienced driver. Not to worry about money since he could fix all that with the Amsterdam office . . . It was as urgent as that? It was indeed.

He clumsily packed a bag one-armed, then he picked up

the phone, once more uncertain. On an impulse he rang Margaret Seyer. She didn't answer at once and he almost hung up. At last he heard her say: 'Hullo?'

'I'm going to Amsterdam,' he said.

'Again?' She knew he went often and wasn't interested. There was a pause. 'I've just come back from father.'

'How was he?'

'Dying,' she said, 'but dying peacefully.' If she was crying he couldn't hear her.

'I'm desperately sorry. I . . . Goodbye.'

She caught a note in his voice which she'd never heard. 'What do you mean, "Goodbye" like that?'

'Just goodbye.'

The car arrived as he finished talking. The driver took Peter's bag to it, then they slipped smoothly into the main traffic at Lancaster Gate. The little red Alfa followed but not so smoothly. It had in fact missed an accident as a biggish grey car forced its way across its bows. The grey car took station behind the Daimler where it held it.

A watchful forty yards behind Martiny Dominy reached for the radio . . . Mr. Laver was out? God blast and damn. Not that it made much difference now, there wasn't time for official action. Dinoba could come and go as he pleased. He could, that is, if the grey car let him.

In the grey car they had a radio too and its user was talking to Striped Tie curtly. 'Dinoba's now in an office car. He has a bag. They're driving towards the airport too.'

'How far ahead is the car with Dolan?'

'He was picked up sharp at four o'clock. They'll be at the airport now and waiting.'

'Could Dinoba make Dolan's flight as well?'

'If they tread on it. They're treading on it.'

'See that he doesn't get on to it.'

'Right.'

'And see that Jacky Dolan does.'

'He's got two men with him already, remember.'

'Who are not expecting Dinoba behind. Whatever he's got in mind and we don't know that.'

'So if Dinoba tries to interfere—'

'You'd better make sure he gets no chance.'

13

The big grey saloon tailed the office Daimler and the Alfa was tailing the big grey saloon. Martin Dominy was uneasy, for there were far too many unknowns for safe deduction and therefore for effective planning. What facts there were were simple but inconclusive: Dinoba was in an office car which was driving towards an airport, and Dominy had noticed that a bag had been put in the Daimler's boot. *Ergo* he meant to catch a plane since he wouldn't have taken a bag with him if he'd simply been meaning to meet an arrival. No marks for that one, either from Laver (Martin still couldn't reach him) or certainly not from Charles Russell who'd taught him to think. It was better to think of the big grey car, of the two men in it he hadn't recognized. If thinking were a proper word for what was really a choice of guesses.

But one thing wasn't a guess by now—he could safely assume whom the two men worked for. True, but what work? They could be going to the airport on what amounted to a reconnaissance, simply to check Dinoba's movements, to report where he'd gone and to leave it at that. There was nothing in logic to rule that out, but to Dominy, a hard old hand, it fell very far short of convincing. There were a dozen ways of checking on movements short of tailing a man in a car on a highway, and once you'd accepted Paul Frei in the background you must also accept that his agents would be professionals.

So the men in the grey saloon weren't just making a recce; they meant to take action, probably to prevent Dinoba leaving the country. Assuming they couldn't persuade him that could mean violence, quite possibly serious, but Dominy was too experienced to rule out an even chance of it. If Paul Frei thought the stakes were high enough . . .

So assume that affairs had so developed that Peter Dinoba

must stay in England. But then Frei or his agent or both of them would on form have foreseen the development; there were various things they could do and several nasty, which was one of the reasons Martin himself had been put on to watching Peter Dinoba, but forethought and careful planning were the hallmarks of Frei and the men he used, instead of which here were two unknown strongarms chasing another car with Dinoba in it. That would be amateurish unless whatever made it necessary were both unforeseen and urgently unacceptable. Frei wouldn't have overlooked the chance that Peter Dinoba might go abroad since he often did and Frei would know it, and if that hadn't suited him Frei would have taken firm steps to prevent it. Therefore he didn't mind Peter just leaving, he minded his leaving here and now, perhaps even by a particular plane.

Martin Dominy fought his immediate problem which was simply what he should do in a pinch. He was persuaded now that this was serious; he wasn't armed but he didn't regret it. Shooting it out at an airport was never on.

The grey car had closed on the Daimler now and Dominy closed up in turn. They went through the tunnel nose to tail then, skirting the roundabout, separated. The Daimler and the grey car found a space between two airport buses, Martin Dominy one in the parallel lane. He could watch from there and he did so. The chauffeur took Peter Dinoba's bag and the two of them went to check it in. One man left the grey car, the other drove on (He'll have to park but then he'll come back.) The chauffeur came out without the bag and the dignified Daimler drove away.

Martin Dominy climbed out quickly. A parking attendant protested at once but he gave him two pounds and a level stare. This wasn't a proper policeman and he wouldn't know Dominy's name or Warrant. Martin Dominy looked at his watch as he ran. It was twenty past five, they were cutting it fine.

At the top of the little escalator he looked round the seething Concourse. It was the usual depressing chaos, an area built for one order of traffic now hopelessly trying to handle another. Once they'd kept you here in the waiting bays till your flight was almost ready to go, then filtered you forward through Passport Control to the comparative calm of Departure. Now they'd given that up, you went through as you could. Had Dinoba gone through? Martin Dominy couldn't see him, for this was a rush hour, the Concourse was jammed. He couldn't see much but at least he could hear and a female voice was braying brassily through the speakers. 'B.E.A. regret to announce that their flight B.E. Four-Three-Four to Amsterdam will be delayed. This is due to operational difficulties.'

. . . Not 'due to', woman, you mean 'because of', and of course you don't regret it at all. Nobody's made an actual mistake, everyone's got a perfect answer. So why should you even sound regretful? The customer is always wrong.

In any other circumstances the bland insolence would have maddened him but the news the voice bore was for once not unwelcome. If the flight was delayed so was Peter Dinoba; he might not be in Departure yet, and in the sweating mill of bodies was an element of safety. It was the worst airport in Europe but for the first time Martin was glad of it.

He stood on tiptoe, peering anxiously, then tried to force a passage through the press. There were other delays and a backlog of flights, and movement was very hard work indeed. All the world was here and perhaps his wife, a babel of every tongue known to man. Martin Dominy ground his teeth and pushed. He had to get to the waiting bays and every race in the world seemed determined he shouldn't. The tourists were the worst, he knew, in parties of twenty or more and prone to panic. One had just done so, rushing like unnerved hens to the first enclosure then, inexplicably, changing their minds and pouring out. The rabble caught him aflank, a chatter of high-pitched worried voices, pushing him discourteously against a showcase displaying he cared not what. He grabbed for support but for a second he could see. The first enclosure was thinner now and Dominy fought his way in dourly. Peter Dinoba wasn't there but some of the crowd was sitting down and Martin at last could see across it. Dinoba was two bays off and not alone.

It took Dominy nearly a minute to get there but less than a second to sum it up. Dinoba was sitting tense and grim, and Peter Dinoba knew something was wrong. He was looking from time to time at the man beside him. Who wore an elegant beard, not the ill-kept badge of protest but in fact to hide a knife scar. Beard wasn't returning Dinoba's glances but was looking at the entrance hard, giving a small but acknowledging nod as the man who had parked the car forced his way in. There wasn't a vacant seat for him but he pushed himself slowly across to the other. There he stopped and stood solidly, facing Dinoba.

Martin Dominy started to work out the chances. Departure would be no haven of ease with the backlog of flights what it seemed to be, so Peter had taken a seat where he found it and later he'd move when they called his flight. He would, that is, if the two men let him.

Which left Dominy wondering where and how. The where, he decided, could only be here. If his reasoning had been in any way right then this was a job laid on in haste, so they'd hardly have thought of passports and tickets and without them they wouldn't get through to Departure. Then they'd pull it in here or not at all and Dinoba looked a pushover; he had an arm in a sling, he was evidently in pain, so they'd work it as an accident. When his flight was called Dinoba would rise, there'd be a move for the door and the first man would trip him. He'd trip him so that he fell on that arm, blocking the other to make quite sure. Then the other would trip on Dinoba in turn and he'd know how to do it perfectly. First the crippling screwing heel in the lumbar vertebrae, then the hand put out to save himself, the thumb in the eye as Dinoba writhed. Martin Dominy knew for he'd seen it done.

He lit a cigarette and waited, knowing he might have to wait some time. When Heathrow had one of its frequent shambles he had waited for hours and once for a day.

He was finishing his third cigarette when the brassy voice started to bray again. B.E.A. were announcing that passengers for the Amsterdam flight should proceed at once and damn their eyes . . .

He didn't wait for the cocky voice to end but edged the standing man sharply aside and took his place. To Dinoba he said deliberately, loudly enough for all three to hear:

'Mr. Peter Dinoba? You're in trouble—I think you know it.'

Dinoba didn't answer him. He trusted nobody now, no white man especially.

'You don't know me and my name doesn't matter.' Dominy raised his voice a tone to make sure that the others heard him. 'I work in the Security Executive. You may have heard of it.' He could see that Peter Dinoba had. 'Will you trust me?'

There was a silence. Peter looked at the strongarms—they hadn't moved; he looked hard at Martin Dominy, hard but he'd made his mind up. 'I haven't another choice,' he said.

'Then listen very carefully. They're going to maim you in a faked accident, and I'm going to try to stop them. When you get up I'll move behind you. Don't worry if you feel me touching, I'll be very close behind indeed. But if anything happens stand still at once. The important thing is not to fall.'

'I understand.'

'Then get up quietly.'

Peter Dinoba rose at once.

'I'm behind you now. Walk to the exit steadily. Watch out.'

The two of them began to move. Martin Dominy felt one man behind him and the knowledge made his scalp crawl. He could do nothing with that if they'd accept the risk of clubbing him, but his hope was that they'd work on their drill. That drill would be for an accident, not for a public fracas with a man who now knew that any accident wouldn't be one. Moreover he'd have to be dealt with first and he'd meant them to hear the Executive's name. It hadn't the reputation that assaults on its staff were soon forgotten.

It was hard to forget the man behind him but Martin was watching the second closely. The man with the beard was level with Peter, not shoulder to shoulder but a woman between them. She was middle-aged and distinctly stout, Martin couldn't have chosen a better block. Four paces to the door still, one, two, three . . .

The woman pushed suddenly, rudely, in front. Peter and Beard were touching now. Beard put his hand in his pocket. His face was stone.

'I wouldn't do that.'

Martin's hand was in his pocket too though it didn't hold more than a clean silk handkerchief. It wouldn't be an accident now, it could only be a cosh or worse. Martin couldn't be sure Beard wouldn't risk it. He was hesitating, there was one more step . . .

With a single compulsive push they were through and for the first time Martin Dominy turned. They were through and they were through alone. Martin pulled out the clean silk handkerchief, wiping his hands deliberately. He wasn't ashamed the palms were sweating. Peter Dinoba said quietly:

'Thank you.'

'Explanations come later, we haven't time here. So just listen again. Unless they've got passports and tickets you're safe enough. I don't think they'll have either or they'd have followed us in here by now. Just the same I'll see you on to the plane. I haven't a ticket either but I've a card which should get me through to it. And the passport people know me a bit.'

'You're very efficient,' Dinoba said.

'I get into trouble whenever I'm not. So I'll see you catch that plane and that's my job.'

At the steps of the aircraft they shook hands silently, and five minutes later Martin Dominy was in the Concourse again. The other two men had disappeared, but there was still a loose end and he meant to tie it. He went to the booth marked B.E.A. and asked to see the passenger list—yes, the B.E.A. flight to Amsterdam. Four-Three-Four—he'd just seen it leave. There was the usual official We-Can't-Do-That, a conditioned and purposeless fuss since such lists weren't secret, but Martin was given the list in the end. He looked at it and he looked again . . . Mr. James Arthur Dolan, one-way ticket to Schipol. One way.

. . . And that had been important enough to make sure that Dinoba should not go too. Probably Jacky had blocks on him, but the passenger list wouldn't show which they were. In any case Laver would do the thinking.

Martin went back to his car at the double. There was a ticket behind the wiper and he allowed himself a rueful grin. So a couple of quid had not been enough. He drove through the tunnel and found a layby, then he reached again for the radio . . . Mr. Laver was out still? Damn the man. Then give me a stenographer, please, and make sure the channel doesn't break down on us.

He began to dictate his first report.

Margaret Seyer was fighting a doubting conscience, knowing that she'd done little wrong but also that she'd done nothing right. There were excuses perhaps, but she was much too proud to make them. She'd had an appointment to see her father and she hadn't been sure she'd find him alive, but now she knew the worst and it wasn't so bad. The doctor hadn't hesitated, for she wasn't the sort of woman you lobbed along. Her father might last a week or a month: the important thing was he was happy at last, when his time came to die he'd be dying in peace.

So she'd thought of her father first and that hadn't been wrong, but she needn't have been so callous with Peter Dinoba. He'd come to her in a personal crisis, and now she'd had time to think she could share it. But when it had mattered she'd brushed it aside, all she'd cared for had been her father's guilt. And now he was scot of that but she wasn't. A man had come to her in extremity and she'd sent him away with comfortless words. A woman didn't do that if she wished to remain one.

She picked up the phone and rang Peter Dinoba. The number rang out and she waited ten minutes. She dialled again, and again without answer. Half an hour later a third time. Nothing.

. . . He'd had his arm in a sling and Victor Lomax was dead.

She started to form Richard Laver's number but as the call came through she changed her mind. Richard Laver was a cousin of sorts so she'd go to him and talk directly. At once. She'd always thought of him with a real respect for he wasn't the typical civil servant. He wouldn't, she realized, be where he was if he'd simply been a Minute-writer. He could be calm, sometimes maddeningly, but he was a practical, even hard-bitten man with a host of interests outside his work and not all of them intellectual. He was certainly calm as she told him her story. 'I let Peter down,' she said. 'I dropped him flat.'

'Perhaps.' She liked it that he made none of her own excuses about her father, and though he must know that she wouldn't have come if Dinoba had meant nothing to her he didn't consider it worth a mention. People would have their more intimate problems, people would solve them as best they could. But he was clearly willing to help in this one. He was saying, quiet as ever:

'I know most of what you've just told me.'

'You do?' He didn't take umbrage easily and forgave her that she'd barked at him.

'We had an interest of our own in Peter. I'm afraid I can't tell you what just yet, but I'll give you some information. You thought he was going to Amsterdam. I know he has.'

She didn't ask how he knew or why. 'With his arm in a sling?'

'Yes, that was reported.'

'Oh God,' she said, 'I'd like a drink.'

He gave her one unfussily. 'Do you know where he usually stays there?'

'At the Doelen.'

He made a quick note and waited for Margaret. 'I can guess what you're thinking,' she said at length; she looked up at him fiercely. 'If he did kill Victor Lomax then he killed my father's murderer. Not legally perhaps, but Lomax killed him.'

'I'd thought of that myself, you know.'

'Then what are you going to do?
'I'm going to Amsterdam,' he said.
'You think you could help?'
'Perhaps.'
'But what can you do?'
'Very little myself but we've got friends in Amsterdam.'

He was thinking that it was perfectly true: he had indeed good friends in Amsterdam. One of several things which had surprised him in the Executive was that within forty-eight hours of his arrival at Charles Russell's desk a dozen letters had been delivered to it and all of them in similar terms. Ten of them had been beautifully typed and two had been written out in hand. They had come from every major country and from one which had astonished him. All had wished him well in his new appointment, no doubt deserved, and all had hoped ardently that co-operation would continue. He'd been flattered but not deceived for a minute. Co-operation would be forthcoming just so long as there was mutual interest. When there wasn't they wouldn't know his name.

He heard Margaret say sharply: 'Have you telephoned to your friends yet?'

He still didn't relish her manner but could see she was under unbearable strain. 'That isn't a secret—yes, I've rung them.'

'When are you going?'
'Half-nine tomorrow.'
'I'm coming too,' she said at once.
'I'd rather you didn't. What could you do?'
'I don't know that but I know I'm going.'
'And your father?' he asked.
'The latest is that he may last some time. There's nothing I can do for him now, the important thing is he's happy again.'

'I've got friends in Amsterdam. Have you?'

'No,' she said, 'only Peter.'

Another call had been going to Amsterdam from Striped Tie
and Paul Frei had been receiving it with an annoyance which
years of discipline hid. The last thing he wanted was an
African on Jacky's heels, particularly an African who'd had
close contact with Mervin Seyer; he had gone to some pains
over Peter Dinoba, seeing him as a possible danger, but
Striped Tie had failed to neutralize him. Striped Tie had an
excuse of course, and had pressed it on the phone persuasively: the Executive had intervened and he hadn't had
Frei's authority to risk an open conflict with the Executive.
Paul Frei was fair-minded and saw the point, but decided at
once that it wasn't the real one. If the Executive had now
come in then Jacky was in instant danger, and they'd been
protecting Dinoba at London airport so it wasn't incon-
ceivable that the man was actually working for them. Even
if he wasn't he could certainly be a nuisance, and this wasn't
a happy moment for uncovenanted nuisances. It was still a
first rule to minimize risks and Frei proceeded to do so
deliberately. He cut Tie off a trifle brusquely . . . No, he
didn't require his services in Amsterdam of all places on
earth.

He thought for ten minutes, then sent for his secretary.

The flight next morning was punctual for once, and
Laver and Margaret Seyer walked up the covered ramp at
Schipol. A little different, both were thinking, from the
shameful chaos of Heathrow. They went through Passport
Control and on into Customs, and both were facing the
bench as a polite voice said behind them:

'Mr. Laver?'

They turned.

'Permit me to introduce myself.' The English was excellent, the bow rather formal. 'My name is de Kuyper.'

'Mr. Commissioner, how do you do.' Laver knew that de Kuyper had a much longer title, something which, freely translated, meant State Commissioner for Matters happening Internally of an Undesirable Nature. He also knew that Mr. Commissioner would do. He turned towards Margaret. 'Miss Margaret Seyer—Mr. Commissioner de Kuyper.' It was all a trifle ponderous but so were the official Dutch. Laver thought none the less of them for it.

'Enchanted,' de Kuyper said; he returned to Laver. 'Miss Seyer? You mentioned her father in that most interesting telephone call.'

'Also a Mr. Dolan and Mr. Dinoba.'

'Both have arrived. Mr. Dolan has been taken to the house which you suggested.'

'And Mr. Dinoba?'

There was a second's silence. 'I am afraid I have a surprise for you.' De Kuyper was clearly not at ease. 'I fear perhaps an unwelcome one.'

Margaret said savagely: 'Tell me.'

'Peter Dinoba has disappeared.'

14

Peter Dinoba was thinking again. He had gone to Lomax in blind emotion and the result, for Victor Lomax, had been the final of all disasters, death; he knew from Margaret Seyer that Jacky had been to her father and that her father was now composed to die; he had gone to Jacky for information and his wife had given it freely, almost too freely. So Jacky D had picked Seyer's brains and had gone to Amsterdam to sell his knowledge. It didn't increase Dinoba's fear that someone had thought an attempt worth while to prevent his own departure there, but it increased his already desperate sense that the whole affair was now at a crisis. Jacky had been to Seyer, Seyer had talked; Jacky had gone to Amsterdam and he'd never been there in his life before. The evangelist Jacky D was finished but the other James Dolan had something to sell.

Peter's arm was a flaming agony now but in spite of it his mind was working. Amsterdam was no strange and unknown city, de Masseys had an office there and Peter Dinoba friends in it, one in particular, a senior in the firm whom Peter trusted, a man with a brave career in Resistance which he'd never been known to talk about but which Peter had heard of and much admired. He was respectable now and active in politics, but a man with his contacts in more worlds than one. Peter intended to tell him the truth, then to ask him the simple and vital questions: who in this city where Jacky had come at no notice at all—who was big enough and ruthless enough to be interested in S.P.D.? Who had a motive and who would dare? There couldn't, Peter Dinoba was sure, be more than one or two at the most. After that it was clear though it might not be easy, but Jacky would go to his contact and there he'd be found. Peter had an ancient pistol though he'd never yet fired it and hadn't expected to.

It surprised him that he felt no emotion, only a driving sense of duty. Once he'd loved Jacky—that almost amused him. Now he was empty of feeling, a man with a mission. To kill Jacky would give him no personal pleasure, it would simply be obligation discharged. As for his own life, it wasn't important. Moreover it was already forfeit, forfeit to the English police. He'd killed a man in self-defence but the man had been white and Peter was black. To the Peter Dinoba who sat in the aircraft the inescapable fact of his colour was the single stone he could cling to in the darkness which was now his world.

Jacky Dolan was sitting three rows in front, a straight-backed man on either side, and at Schipol airport Dinoba watched them. They were met by a big black car and driven away. Peter didn't interfere with it for he was thinking again and sensibly. It would be possible to shoot here and now but also it would be self-defeating. Jacky had come here to make a contact and that contact must at least be found. Once he was known there'd be people prepared to deal with him: Margaret's friends in the Executive would be the first in a line which Peter believed would be both long and sufficiently powerful. So he must have the name but also he must have it quickly. For he alone could silence Jacky. Give Jacky too long to talk and the evil, the dreadful thing was done. Knowledge was of the essence but so was time.

Though Peter didn't know it Paul von Frei held the same opinion. Dinoba could be an embarrassment but only for a limited time, in fact till Frei's experts arrived next day. That limited time was important, though, and Paul von Frei had covered it.

So Peter watched the black car drive off and by eight o'clock was booking in at the Doelen. As usual, and deservedly, the Doelen was full to bursting, but like all good hotels it could always find that magical room for a really valued customer. An American had a night flight out and reckoned to get some sleep before he left, but if Mr. Dinoba could somehow amuse himself till midnight . . .

He said that he could and went to a chemist; he needed something to ease his pain and he knew now his arm was serious. That would have to come later if ever the question arose at all, but meanwhile he couldn't afford to collapse. On the way to the chemist he called his friend's house . . . No, he was out with his wife at the opera and afterwards there was a supper party. It was a blow, a night wasted, but it might have been worse. Peter's friend would be in his office next day and by a quarter to nine at the latest. He was a senior man but that was his time. This wasn't London.

Peter bought his analgesic and used it, once, in the shop, what the chemist advised, then a second and equal dose outside. He stood on the steps and grimly thought. He had four hours to kill, and even when his bed was free he knew he'd find no sleep in it. He felt far too sick for food or drink, and for something to do walked down to the Old Grass-market quay. The tourist launches were mostly moored but it was a fine clear evening and one was leaving. To fill the time he bought a ticket, though he'd made the canal-tour a score of times. The launch wasn't full, he found a seat at the side, thinking it strange that a man should choose to sit next to him when there were other and better seats still free.

They slipped out into the Amstel river. Peter was light-headed now, partly a double dose of drug which was fighting his pain but clouding his mind, partly the matchless magic of an evening on lighted water. The sharp swords of the street lights swept the river before it shattered them, the glow from the windows of ancient buildings made quiet pools for the bows of the launch to destroy. It had always seemed half unreal to Peter and tonight it was purest fantasy. Absurd red electric light bulbs had been strung round the arch of every bridge, and he stared at them half-hypnotized, watching them merge, then part again, trying to bring them in focus, failing.

They went under the Blue Bridge, then right into the Herengracht, and the student-guide began her *spiel* in English, Dutch and German . . . These had been the houses of prosperous merchants, were now the homes of the very rich. You could tell how rich the owner was by the number of flights of steps to the house. Three flights was a multi-millionaire, two flights a very rich man indeed, one flight just ornery stinking rich. A pause for happy laughter which astonishingly came. The British passengers would no doubt note that their consulate still had a pair of flights.

Peter Dinoba paid scant attention. For one thing he'd heard all this before and for another his mind was wandering . . . Somewhere down this superb canal would be the house of the man he was seeking. What was the damned girl saying now? A house anywhere in these fine old rows would cost you two million guilders at least. It was a very Dutch state-ment but it happened to be true. Only rich men, rich firms lived here, and only a very rich man or some government behind him . . .

His chin fell on his chest, not in sleep but in unconscious-ness.

He came to as the launch went astern, then bumped, but he wasn't alarmed for it often happened. Indeed the bump told him where they were, out of the Herengracht by now, at the mouth of the Brewers' Canal and waiting. It was always an awkward corner and none but the smallest launches could clear it without reversing. Then they'd go left under the Haarlemmerstraat, into the inner harbour and finally into the real one. There was always some manœuvring here, and tonight there was another vessel, coming against them the opposite way. The helmsman gave her precedence, backing his launch against the wall of the canal. Over the railing three men were watching, and in the street behind was a big black car.

The man at Peter's side stood up, catching the rope which snaked down to him smoothly. Peter wasn't properly conscious yet and in any case the man was expert. The rope went under Peter's armpits and the man threw a sailor's bowline deftly. He held up his hand and the pull came on promptly. One instant Peter was sitting, the next he wasn't. The man caught a second rope and climbed. The student-guide screamed—it was much too late. The big black car was already moving.

Jacky Dolan had often been frightened before but now was quite simply terrified. Striped Tie had talked of his principal but Jacky hadn't met him yet and he'd been locked in these two rooms since his arrival. What he'd met had been a secretary, and Richard Laver had once reflected that private secretaries took their mores from their masters. This one had read Frei wrong though he didn't know it. He'd seen the ruthlessness and was aping it, but he'd taken nothing of the discipline, the occasional flash of self-mocking humour. He was in fact a bully and had much enjoyed bullying Jacky . . . Mr. Dolan had a complaint to make? The food wasn't to his taste perhaps, or the supply of whisky inadequate? The secretary had looked at the bottle contemptuously. It was the second in fifteen hours or so and already there wasn't a great deal left. Such matters could be attended to, but to ask anything else would be most unreasonable. What indeed had Mr. Dolan expected? An immediate interview with a man who would pay a hundred thousand? Surely he must realize that such a man would be a busy one.

The secretary started to turn the knife, relishing it in his horrible way. But perhaps it wasn't quite unreasonable to inquire about the length of his stay. Mr. Dolan was doubtless a busy man too. The teutonic sneer crashed down with a graceless thud. So the secretary could see nothing wrong in relieving the curiosity of so honoured a guest as was Mr. Dolan. Who perhaps would glance from the window. (He had.) It was one-way glass by the way and too thick to break. Outside he would see the Herengracht, and moored by this house a substantial cabin cruiser. If Mr. Dolan were interested it was very unusual to see such a thing, for only a man of real importance could moor overnight in such famous water.

The secretary saw he was frightening Jacky and it amused his mean spirit to frighten him more . . . Mr. Dolan, then, would observe the cruiser, and he would also observe her lines and size. She was in fact sea-going, and with a little extra fuel on board could make considerable trips for considerable periods. One such was contemplated when two scientists flew in from Germany tomorrow. Mr. Dolan should not be astonished to hear that in matters of science proper scientists were essential. Then they would all take a pleasant cruise together, perhaps through the North Sea Canal itself but more likely into the Zuider Zee. There was a great deal of room in the Zuider Zee, room to talk and for other things too. After that . . .

After that who knew? *Auf Wiedersehen.*

As the secretary left him Jacky D heard the lock snap. He went straight to the bottle, not terrified now but in total panic. Unknowingly he began to pray. Our Father which art in Heaven . . . He broke off abruptly. His ex-God wouldn't hear him and why indeed should he? This wasn't God's doing but Jacky Dolan's. He'd told himself he was out of his league, he'd warned himself he'd be walking blind. It wasn't as though he'd been threatened either, just a hint from

that lawyer that he knew about Anna Vescovi, a plain statement of fact that he wouldn't find other work easy to get.
He'd been classically tempted, he'd classically fallen.

True. But the sheer bad luck of the way it had gone, the
speed things had happened! If Doris hadn't made that crisis,
if that nursing home hadn't telephoned when it did. Had the
lawyer-man known of that or even fixed it? Jacky would
never know now and it didn't matter. They hadn't
threatened him, no, but nor had they given him time to
think. The draft could have been stopped, the bait pulled
back. So he'd swallowed it like a foolish fish and they still
had the barb in his choking throat.

He took another neat whisky to dull his terror. When
things happened at this pace you went with the stream, you
went with it or not at all. He'd thought that before,
deceiving himself for not using his judgement. So the stream
had washed him helplessly into this comfortable but prison
flat—living-room, bedroom, bathroom, unlimited booze.
And one-way glass too thick to break and a lock on the
door, outside, which he couldn't see. In the canal below a
large cabin cruiser and beyond the canal a waste of sea. Two
scientists coming from Germany . . .

Jacky D had been pacing the room but stopped dead.
They'd question him of course, but he didn't mind that.
After all they had bought him for just that purpose. But
when he'd given them all he knew, what then? The promised
second fifty thou and a ticket back to London? Possible—
barely possible. But also, he realized now, unlikely. He'd
still have his knowledge whatever he told them and they
wouldn't wish that, would barely accept it. *What motive
would they have to let him live?* Put like that there was one
answer. He finished the bottle, lay down on the bed. He
began to sweat miserably.

When Peter came to he was lying in a surgery. He knew from the smell for his eyes were bandaged. Someone was holding his good arm and talking. 'It won't hurt at all, I promise you that much. Just a prick in the arm and no more pain.'

15

Margaret Seyer and Richard Laver were waiting in the Commissioner's outer office. He was a tactful man and hadn't offered them a lift in his own car from Schipol, putting a second at their private disposal. He had realized that they would wish to talk and they would wish to do it without him. They had, he'd thought coolly, the right to that before they met him on his official home ground, and Margaret in particular had used the opportunity. She had insisted that after Peter's disappearance she was in this affair just as much as was the Executive, so she was coming with Richard Laver to Commissioner de Kuyper's office. Richard had tried to dissuade her. What purpose would her presence serve—it might even inhibit de Kuyper? But she had shown her claws unashamedly: she meant to come and he couldn't stop her. That was the simple fact of it. She knew enough now to bring down the pillars and if he didn't agree she'd pull on them. There were newspapers, both Dutch and English . . .

For a moment he'd thought she was bluffing but not for long. He'd always thought her formidable, not a woman to take a chance with. Nevertheless, in the outer office, he was still trying hard to dissuade her. 'Leaving blackmailing me aside,' he was saying, 'how do you think you can help Dinoba?'

'I didn't say I could. Only that I've the right to know.'

'I could tell you what happens.'

'You *could*.'

'You're as hard as nails,' Richard Laver said. He spoke without resentment, even with a reluctant respect.

She managed the shade of her usual smile. 'You'd be surprised how nails bend.'

'But not when you hammer them?'

'Not good nails—no. Maybe when you hang things on them.'

'A man, for instance?' he asked, but she didn't answer, and a secretary, most official, showed them in. De Kuyper was very hospitable, offering them the gin which bore his name, making a little joke about wishing he owned such a profitable brand. He was hospitable and courteous, but Richard could see that he was playing at home and knew it. A few days ago he had written a letter and that letter had offered co-operation, but Richard Laver knew at once that he didn't intend to give it, or very little.

So the Commissioner had received Mr. Laver's telephone call and following it a coded telegram, and of course he'd been very disturbed indeed. There'd been a heavy pause and a very Dutch stare. But it was difficult to see what his country could do. It wasn't as though this were a matter of NATO, something to do with radar or even nuclear. In such a matter he wouldn't have hesitated. But no, this was something extremely distasteful which Her Majesty's Government and no doubt the Americans had allowed to be born when most doctors would have strangled it. Most Dutch doctors, at any rate. He would put it to his Ministers if Mr. Laver insisted but was confident there could be only one answer. That would come in five words: Keep out at all costs.

Richard Laver was uneasy, the new boy and aware of it, wishing it were Charles Russell who sat in his place. Charles Russell could have dealt with this for Russell had the experience; he'd have done this stolid Dutchman some personal service, or he'd have known all about that affair down in Limburg long before the Commissioner had reached that rank or anything like it, indeed he'd have put the bite on him as Margaret Seyer had just squeezed Richard. He'd have carried the guns and Laver didn't, or more accurately he lacked the tools. He'd been reckoned a good negotiator once, but this wasn't that sort of negotiation. What this Dutchman was saying was all too true. Richard Laver said, fishing:

'And Paul von Frei?'

Ah, that made it even more delicate. The Commissioner wouldn't conceal from them that he mistrusted von Frei for many good reasons, but that was his private opinion, not an official's. Frei was a citizen of the Netherlands now, and though de Kuyper believed a mistake had been made (he put it no higher, Mr. Laver would follow) he was now a very important one. He had the ear of Persons in the Highest of Places, people known for their passion for property in all forms, from airlines and petroleum downwards; he ran, and from Holland, one of Europe's great combines; he brought in much money, he gave much employment, and all these things counted heavily. Frei wasn't a man to be harried or leant on. The first sign of either and de Kuyper would be out.

This, Laver knew, was true again, and again it wouldn't have been decisive if de Kuyper had wished it shouldn't be. Richard was on poor ground for a serious fight but decided a probe could do no harm.

'You're denying von Frei is behind all this?'

'By no means. Since Mr. Dolan has gone to his house I'm prepared to agree your theory fits.'

'You're extremely frank.'

'Then permit me to be franker. Have you a shred of evidence that I or the police could act on?'

'None.'

'Then you put my position perfectly. I deplore this Selective Pigmentation Disease and my government would use stronger language. I fear that Paul Frei has disgraceful plans, but even if you established it I should still have to go to my Ministers.'

Margaret Seyer had been listening with an evident impatience. Laver didn't like the look of her. She said sharply, a naked demand:

'And Peter Dinoba?'

The Commissioner looked at her. 'I told you, madam, he's disappeared.' De Kuyper's manner was now very formal and Richard was scarcely blaming him. 'I could tell you that at the airport since we'd checked that he'd booked at the Doelen from midnight but never returned to take up his booking. But the how of his disappearance will be a matter for the police, and I was not prepared to tell you that till the police had decided their line of action.' There was an unmistakable stress on the pronoun you, a bow towards Richard Laver, rather pointedly for him alone. 'There is protocol in the country and I do not regret it.'

'For Christ's sake cut the cackle.'

Richard said: 'Steady. Steady, please.'

De Kuyper ignored the interruption. 'Since my colleagues the police have no objection, yes, I will do just that.' He reflected, compressing his thoughts; finally he said stiffly: 'At round about ten o'clock last night a man was abducted, snatched quite literally, from a boat-cruise around the inner canals. The man was an African.'

Margaret was on her feet at once. 'Didn't you have a man on him?'

The Commissioner had his temper still but only by a fraying edge. 'Yes, madam, I did. I had a man in that launch but I regret it was too well organized. Too fast.'

It was typical, Richard Laver thought, that she didn't query this or fuss. Instead she said:

'Then Paul Frei's got him.'

'I'm obliged to admit it's possible.'

'You know it,' she said.

'Madam, I do *not* know it. Nor do the police. You may accept my assurances that they will do everything humanly possible. Possible under our law, may I also add.'

She said something about Dutch law and Richard sighed. If she heard him she paid no attention. 'Days, perhaps weeks to trace these men, and even if you catch them why should they talk? A man who employed them, another behind him. Miles beyond, in the shadows, Paul Frei, quite untouched.' She wasn't weeping but coldly furious. 'Meanwhile—'

'Meanwhile I could hope to serve you a little.' He'd been writing on a visiting card and now passed it to her across the desk. 'That is my personal card to the Chief of Police. You may rely on his assistance in any matter which is a common crime. In any case he is most anxious to meet you.' De Kuyper stood up. 'And now you must really excuse me.' He bowed formally at Margaret Seyer, shook hands with a smile with Richard Laver. 'I look forward to our next meeting. In any other matter but this deplorable Anglo-American germ I should hope to be much more useful.'

In the taxi back to her quiet hotel Richard was silent, depressed and defeated. Richard Laver's first case, he thought ironically—it hadn't been a distinguished one. He'd been to the chief of Dutch Security and the chief had declined to help him. Richard Laver was a fair-minded man and he didn't resent what de Kuyper had done. Come to think of it he'd have chosen the same if their positions had been reversed. Selective Pigmentation Disease wasn't something with which to embroil yourself lightly, and the Dutchman's disgust had been both genuine and justified. Not that that helped Richard Laver whose own masters had blindly allowed the disaster.

He looked sideways at Margaret Seyer, bolt upright and

tense . . . An extraordinary woman, a tycoon *manqué*, or the great commander that Marshal wasn't. But he didn't want a great commander, he wanted Mary Laver, his wife. She wouldn't be able to help him but she'd certainly offer comfort. He needed that badly for he knew what he must do; he hadn't in practice the option since the storm was now inevitable. It was better to leave with dignity, so he'd go back to England tomorrow and he'd talk to Harry Tuke at once. He'd offer his resignation and Harry Tuke would be bound to accept it.

He turned to Margaret Seyer beside him. 'You certainly put de Kuyper's back up.' He could speak without overt anger still but his manner had an edge she couldn't miss.

She didn't but parried it wickedly. 'He was just another official,' she said.

He let it pass—in a sense he deserved it. Nor in fact had she prejudiced de Kuyper's decision, for he'd declined to help in the larger matter well before Margaret had snapped his Dutch head off. Richard Laver frowned, annoyed but fighting for understanding.

'Would you like me to come to the police with you?'

'I'm not going to the police,' she said.

'I think you're mistaken. They could even make you.'

'Let them do as they please.' She gave him a sudden smile which surprised him. It was relaxed, even friendly—she'd made her decision. 'Tell me,' she said, 'you know all about Paul Frei.'

'I wish we could say that or anything like it.'

'But you've a file on him?'

'Of course we have.'

'Then where does he live? And how?'

'He has a house in the country which he uses mostly for entertaining. Another on the Herengracht where he lives.'

'Do you happen to know the phone number?'

He stared at her, shaken. 'Don't be a bloody fool,' he said.

When Peter recovered consciousness he was lying in an ordinary bed and the surgery smell was wholly absent. His arm was outside the counterpane, no longer in a sling but lightly bandaged. He could see it since the blindfold had gone; he could also see a bald man bending over him. The bald man said pleasantly:

'Feeling better?'

'Yes, thank you.'

'Permit me to introduce myself. I'm Paul von Frei's personal doctor. That means I am also a good one.'

'Who's Paul von Frei?'

The doctor told him at some length.

'I see,' Peter said. He didn't entirely but it had started to fit. 'Is this von Frei's house?'

'It is.'

'Why was I brought here?'

The doctor said stolidly: 'I can't tell you that. With perfect truth I do not know. You weren't here when I left at eight last night, and I was summoned by telephone to attend a man with a gangrenous wound.' He pointed at Peter's bandaged arm. 'Who did that?'

Peter didn't answer him.

'I don't mean the wound, I can see it was a bullet. I was asking who treated it.'

'A doctor.'

'A doctor!' The bald man looked incredulous. 'A qualified doctor?'

'Yes, I suppose so.'

'God in heaven.' The doctor considered, then finally said disgustedly: 'The wound wasn't actually gangrenous but in a couple of days it might have been. Then you'd have lost

158

your arm—the lot.'

'Thank you,' Peter Dinoba said.

'My job . . . No more pain?'

Peter hadn't realized it yet but for the first time for days
he was free of pain. 'No,' he said, 'and thanks again.'

'You'll have to be careful for quite a bit. That sling was a
scandal, the dressing an outrage. I'll change the present one
from time to time but for the moment it's better to leave it.
You can move your arm when you feel like it, in fact it's
better you should a bit. But you're not to do anything with
it. I'll look after the rest.'

'I'm going to be here some time, then?'

'Medically speaking, no, not at all. Providing your
dressing is properly changed—'

'And not speaking medically?'

'I don't know that, I'm Paul Frei's doctor. Naturally I
attend his guests.'

'Do many come in with septic arms?'

The doctor laughed. 'It's usually much more mundane
than that. They eat too much or more often drink, or they're
elderly and do foolish things. Paul von Frei is very hospitable—very.' The doctor was mildly enjoying his joke,
rather proud that von Frei thought of everything for his
guests. 'Now there's a man upstairs who's been drinking too
much, so I just did the usual things for him. Odd case in its
way. I shouldn't have thought him the drinking type. He
told me he'd been a missionary.'

'That's interesting,' Peter Dinoba said. He was pleased
he was keeping his voice quite steady, but nothing else was
steady, nothing at all . . . So he'd have gone to his ex-
Resistance friend and his friend would have given him Paul
Frei's name. Who had known he was close on Jacky's heels,
had indeed tried to stop him at London airport. So this
Mister Big had acted first, logically and effectively as Mister

Bigs were apt to do. He had Jacky upstairs and Peter down, a Peter in pyjamas, unarmed. If the door wasn't locked there'd be a man on a chair outside it. Peter Dinoba groaned aloud.

'Arm hurting again?' The doctor looked surprised and distressed.

Peter managed a smile, the hardest of his life. 'Not my arm,' he said, 'my self-respect.'

It took Margaret Seyer a full ten minutes to make her contact with Paul von Frei—first a servant, then a junior secretary, then the more senior who had bulled Jacky Dolan. As she moved patiently up the ladder she disclosed her cards in ascending order, her name, then her father's, finally that she was in Amsterdam with the Head of the Security Executive. She'd never lied with any fortitude but considered that 'with' was factual and justified. At last a polite voice answered her . . . Yes, her name was indeed familiar. Mervin Seyer's daughter believed that Paul Frei could in some way help her? It was possible—he would be pleased to try. When should she call? Why at once if that were convenient.

She had expected to be taken to the stereotype of a tycoon's office, the usual props of desk and telephones, the overthick carpet and hanging graphs. Instead she was shown to what was evidently his study. She hadn't the time to observe it in detail but saw at once that Paul Frei had taste. She had once been in Victor Lomax's flat and this was the total opposite. A decorator would have hated it as a jumble of styles and periods, but everything the room held was fine, every article loved by the man who owned it, who rose at once as she came in.

'May I offer you a glass of wine? It's champagne—I often drink it.'

She thought he said it perfectly, without the faintest hint of bombast. He was making a simple statement of fact: the wine was champagne and he liked champagne, what was more he was hoping that she did. It wouldn't be a special treat, something which would impress her. If she said she preferred a gin and tonic he would ring the bell for gin and tonic.

She accepted a glass of wine and sat down. He waited for her to begin to speak, and in the silence, surprisingly easy, she inspected him without seeming to. She found him powerfully attractive. Not physically—he was hideous—but he had an aura of something she'd always admired, the air of a conscious but disciplined power. She didn't doubt he'd be wholly ruthless but whatever he'd be he would never be cruel. For one thing he'd once been a soldier, a good one. But he wasn't a man to fence with or wheedle. She had expected that and had come prepared, saying briskly:

'I've come here to make a proposition.'

He nodded. 'I'm a business man.'

'Give me Peter Dinoba for Jacky Dolan.'

'That's interesting. Please expand a little.'

She felt happier that he made no denials: what she'd always feared was a straight disavowal. He would hardly deny that Jacky Dolan was in this splendid house for he'd been met at the airport and driven here openly, but Peter, if he were here at all, had been kidnapped by night by an organized party. She hadn't a speck of proof he was here, only the practical certainty. It wouldn't have been extraordinary if Frei had met her with flat denial and shown her out.

But he was doing neither, watching her on the contrary with an interest he wasn't concealing. His eyes were half hidden in folds of flesh but they were Baltic blue and very sharp, and there was something behind them she caught at once, an entirely un-Prussian sense of humour. He was saying again:

'Please expand your proposal.'

'Perhaps it sounds crazy but I've something to sell. I can take the Executive off your back.'

'The Security Executive? You mentioned it on the telephone. They employ you?'

She shook her head.

'But you think they're somehow on my back?'

'They're one jump behind you. That could be embarrassing.'

'Are you by any chance trying to frighten me?'

'No.'

He said surprisingly: 'You'd be perfectly justified. I've had dealings with the Executive before. I do not underestimate it, nor the length of its arm.' He was silent a moment, then asked her casually: 'Has anyone ever tried to kill you?'

She shook her head a second time.

'There've been three attempts on my life—no, none by your Executive. The point is I didn't relish them. I'm not ashamed of that at my age. I should like to live a little longer.' He considered, concentrated and formidable. 'But how could you guarantee what you offer?'

'I know too much and I'm ready to use it. I know about S.P.D. though not why you want it.' Margaret leant forward, in her own way as formidable. 'So my government's lumbered with S.P.D., and from my father's visits I'd guess the Americans have it too. They'll want to keep it in the family, to avoid that it's even known it exists. But what could bring down a Minister, perhaps even the Cabinet house of cards, would be if its existence were known *and* known to have slipped to a foreigner. Think of the headlines, the Questions in the House, the demonstrations.'

'I am thinking of them. So?'

'A spark could send up the lot and I hold the matches.'

He began to laugh, quietly at first, then shaking every muscle of his huge frame. When he had himself under control he apologized. 'I wasn't laughing at you but with you—you'll realize that. I very much admire you, Miss Seyer. I hope you're not offended by that. The point is can I believe you?'

'That I'd do as I say? Only you can judge that.'

'Precisely. And I have done so. I have done so without a vestige of doubt . . . May I ask an impertinent question?'

'If it's really impertinent I may not answer.'

'It's the one most women quite wrongly resent . . . How old are you?'

'Twenty-seven,' she said promptly.

'I'm sixty. A pity.'

. . . This astonishing man is propositioning me. What's more I'm not in the least put out. On the contrary I'm rather flattered.

She didn't know his normal speech, hadn't noticed he'd dropped the stiltedness. He was talking now colloquially, relaxedly, with an equal. 'Let's get this straight so there's no mistake. Dolan is essential to me, Dinoba isn't; he's only the threat of an ill-timed nuisance. So I keep Dolan and give you Dinoba. You must take him away from Holland at once. In return you ensure that your own people take no action. You needn't worry about what happens here, the local officials I more or less own. I doubt that your squeeze would work for long but two or three days is all I need. After that I'm on my own but I always have been. Is that the proposition? If so it has attractions for me. Yes?'

'You put it very clearly.'

He said unhesitatingly: 'Done. Now we'll drink to it.'

He picked up a telephone and she heard him order another

bottle. She could see he had drunk a good deal already but he wasn't showing the slightest sign. When the wine came he opened it expertly. There was hardly a pop, no fuss, no frothing. He wasted scarcely a drop of it.

'To your very good health, Miss Margaret Seyer.'

'To your very good health, Herr Baron von Frei.'

For once he didn't protest but smiled. 'That was all a long time ago but some of it sticks. Advantages, if you press me. Not socially but in experience. For instance, I know a proper woman when I see one.'

. . . And what's coming next, the gothic bedroom next door? She had thought of the possibility and had decided to play the hand as it fell. He was ugly but wouldn't slay her; he had the air of experience, he wouldn't be brutal. If that was the part of the price of a life . . .

It was not. Instead he had picked up the house-phone again, talking in rapid incisive German.

'Did you follow that?'

She was pleased he had even supposed she might have. 'Not all of it.'

'I'm not surprised, my doctor is a Bavarian. He has Dinoba in bed but is ready to let him leave at once. When he came here his arm was septic but my doctor has looked after that. Just change the dressings regularly.' He looked at his watch. 'He'll need at least ten minutes to dress. Let us talk for ten minutes.'

'What would you like to talk about?' She was feeling she'd known this man for years.

'Not yourself. If I were an uncertain man I'd find out what I needed to know, which is nothing . . .' He shrugged and laughed, at himself, not embarrassed. 'A pity,' he said again. 'Or it might be.'

'Then may I ask you a question? An impertinent one.'

'What was sauce for the gander.'

'Then why do you want this S.P.D.?'

'I can't tell you that but I'm prepared to defend myself.'
He straightened his back, was suddenly serious. 'Only the
most incompetent government would have allowed such a
thing to creep into the world at all. I haven't a shred of
sympathy for any Minister whose head now rolls.'

'Would you have allowed it?'

'Never.' She believed him entirely. 'But since it exists
I'm entitled to use it.'

She said in German: 'Even the gods fight fools without
hope.'

'Schiller. You still read him?'

'It's all I can remember.'

'And in my view all worth remembering. It makes my
case, though—very neatly.'

'You have one, I think.' It was an admission but offered
happily.

'Hegel would say I'd a very fair case, Nietzsche would say
it was quite conclusive.'

'And that man in California?'

'I don't read amateur philosophers.'

He poured a third glass of wine and she took it. 'I'd like
to give you a present,' he said. 'No, not jewellery—nothing
brash.' He laughed again, a young man's laugh, as his eye
went round the opulent room. 'Are you interested in old
silver?'

'I'm afraid I know nothing about it.'

'A picture?'

'Too much explaining.'

He noticed that she wasn't protesting but was accepting
a gift as what he himself thought it, her proper due, a decent
tribute. He asked a little dubiously: 'Persian carpets?'

'I love them. The one under your chair—you must have stolen it from a museum.'

'You're very nearly right but not quite.' For an instant he looked doubtful again. 'You wouldn't hang it on the wall, by chance?'

'Good heavens, no.'

'Good. Do you know what it is?'

'The dealers call them Isfahans and most of the time they know they're Heratis.'

'You're doubling my pleasure. This is a real one—Shah Abbas's time or thereabouts.' He hauled himself up heavily, pulling away the big armchair; then he knelt and rolled the superlative rug. He looked undignified on the floor and maybe knew it, but it was certain he cared not at all if he did. He was a big one, she'd decided, and in more ways than the obvious. That was the way she admired a man.

'You're giving me a small fortune, you know.'

'What are small fortunes for?' he said.

With the rolled rug under his arm he rose, and the telephone rang and he answered it. 'Peter Dinoba is ready to leave. You'll find a car waiting for you.'

'I don't know how to thank you.'

'A deal. I enjoyed its making.'

'I meant the rug.'

'A rare pleasure.' He went to the door, still holding the rug; he said quietly: 'When Dinoba was brought here he had a gun. He hasn't now.'

'I understand.'

He stood the rolled rug upright, freeing a hand. With it he took hers and kissed it. He did it surprisingly gracefully, then he opened the door on the waiting secretary, handing him the rug to carry.

'Goodbye,' she said.

'Perhaps goodbye.'

He pushed the chair back where the rug had been and sat down in it unathletically . . . An irrelevant difference in ages—what was that? He had known many women and was grateful for their favours. All he'd enjoyed and most despised. He had never even considered marriage, though he'd always wanted a son to bear his name . . . A woman of his own race and class? They were mostly deplorably stupid. The others? He shrugged. He was far too rich to be easily sure. It would have to be a woman he liked, one he trusted and thought an equal. A different sort of equal of course, but the equality was essential. Alas that he'd never met her and at his age he hadn't expected to.

And now he had and her name was Seyer. That could mean less than straight Aryan blood, though it was hard to be sure with English names, but he'd always been contemptuous of theories about names and race. He bred pedigree cattle successfully and had a single but inviolable rule. The dam carried the line and the rest was certain.

He rose and stared at a mirror, reflective . . . By God he was an ugly one, but with a mature intelligent woman that needn't be fatal. He had three stone to lose, though, and that was more serious. He had done it before, he could do it again, but he'd decided he'd comfortably let himself go. Now it was worth the penance again so he'd go to that clinic as soon as he could. His sixty years were no obstacle. He had recent and splendid proof of that but she hadn't been one to breed from.

He looked at the bottle, half-empty now. It was the last he'd be drinking for several weeks so he might as well make the most of it.

When his secretary came in later Frei was peacefully asleep. The secretary saw where the carpet had been and the secretary frowned contemptuously . . . Letting that African go like that, then giving the woman a favourite rug.

There was no fool like an old one, no indeed.

It simply didn't occur to him that he was the mug, not Paul von Frei.

A servant held the door of the car and they climbed into it together. 'To the Doelen, please,' Peter said, then was silent.

To Margaret Seyer the silence was ominous. She hadn't expected effusive thanks, would have cut him short if he'd offered them, but she wasn't prepared for an open hostility. It sprang out of him at furnace heat, withering her and crippling. He said dangerously softly:

'Well?'

'Well what?'

'You know what I mean, don't let's beat about. How did you get me out, please?'

She had expected the question but not so soon. Over supper perhaps, in candlelight, in the glow of wine and maybe more. The glow she felt now was his animal anger.

'How did you get me out, please? Answer.'

She hesitated. It wasn't the moment for explanations, nor one for what he'd called beating about. He said sharply again:

'Answer me.'

'I gave him Jacky Dolan for you. I promised—'

'I can guess what you promised, God damn your soul.'

'But you can't care what happens to Jacky now.'

'Of course I don't, I'm through with Jacky. But you know what Jacky has in his head.'

'I can't be sure.'

He made a gesture, half of weariness, half of frustrated rage. 'Don't lie to me, please, you could spare me that. You know he saw your father and you told me your father was

168

happy at last. Why do you think he's come here at all, to a house like that with a man like Frei?'

'All right,' she said, 'I've been guessing too.'

'Then you know what's going to happen, don't you? They're getting that cabin cruiser ready and I think they mean to sail this evening. Then they'll take her somewhere lonely and pull everything out of Jacky.' He added with total, with shocking indifference: 'Jacky won't come back, of course.'

'Nor would you if you'd gone and I think you were going.'

'So do I and now you've wrecked it all. You've stolen the only chance I had, the only chance to shut Jacky's mouth.'

He was beginning to rasp her nerves and she didn't think. 'What on earth could you do without a gun?'

She saw at once that she'd made a mistake: he was long past reason, the furies rode him. For a moment she thought he was going to strike her.

'So you worked out all the details too! You stole my chance, then you made very sure. They took my gun and they told you so. And you didn't even ask for it back.'

Her temper was rising too, forgivably. 'You're not a gunman and never will be.'

'I shouldn't have been on that boat but they'd left me a knife.'

'For Christ's sake—a pocket-knife! You'd have been guarded day and night and probably tied.' She controlled herself with a painful effort: a man in a rage was bad enough, but if the woman lost her temper too . . . She managed to say neutrally: 'You may be right though I don't think you are. The important point is I got you out. Why do you think I troubled to?'

'How should I know how a white woman thinks?'

'For God's sake stop talking rubbish and listen.'

He said with a bitter contempt which froze her: 'And you thought I'd accept my life like that, on terms which you never told me first.' She started to speak but he silenced her peremptorily, rapping the driver's shoulder hard. 'Stop the car.'

'Peter! Listen—'

'Stop the car.'

They were halfway through the Rembrandtsplein and the driver pulled into the kerb where he could. Peter opened the door and slammed it behind him. She saw him stagger once but recover. Then he began a shaky run, his arm in its clean new bandage swinging. He didn't look back but stumbled on.

Margaret Seyer told the astonished driver to take her to Richard's hotel and fast.

16

Richard Laver was packing glumly, preparing for the evening flight back to London and resignation. He listened to Margaret Seyer with emotions he found it hard to name, even his years of training barely adequate to conceal his surprise. She had never attracted him physically, indeed he found her alarming before desirable, but he had the good civil servant's judicial mind and to this she was talking a foreign language. He'd been successfully married for twenty years, which meant that he held no theories about women. He took them as they came and he was taking this one with difficulty. He wasn't surprised that Paul Frei had done business with her: her proposition had been *realpolitik* and would have appealed to him and amused him too. Besides, if the cruiser were sailing tonight Peter Dinoba could only be an embarrassment, an unwanted body to be disposed of, if necessary permanently. Margaret had promised to take him away, Paul Frei had made a most sensible bargain. As for the Executive, it couldn't in practice have touched him, though it was flattering he had thought it might. Richard Laver hid an ironical smile. He wouldn't wish to play poker with Margaret Seyer.

So none of this astonished Laver but Margaret Seyer's reasoning did. Dinoba had gone running to her, in a panic that S.P.D. was leaking, and all she'd been concerned with had been her father's peace of mind. Understandable? Perfectly, even praiseworthy. But hardly very perceptive. He shook his head crossly—that was typical masculine judgement and therefore suspect. Men attributed certain virtues to women and when they seemed to lack them were stupidly shocked. In any case she had realized it later, coming to Richard Laver penitent, so penitent that she'd followed Peter, hoping to save him from God knew what. In fact she'd probably saved his life but the price she'd paid had been Peter's objective. It had been a hopeless and unrealistic one but that wouldn't be how he'd have seen or would see it. No, one mustn't judge but perhaps one might shrug. No wonder this woman and Paul von Frei had instantly understood each other. They were two of a kind, a natural pair.

Richard Laver sat down on the bed and thought. 'You say they took his gun away? What do you think he means to do?'

'I wish I knew.'

'There's nothing he *can* do. Nothing.'

'Except get himself killed by acting stupidly.'

He considered it unhappily. What she said was almost certainly true. If Dinoba did something silly Frei might be forced to deal with him finally, and Richard's personal failure was big enough already without accepting the risk of another death. He heard himself say uneasily:

'What do you want me to do?'

'The only lead we've got is Frei's house and that cabin cruiser.'

'You're suggesting we go and mount a watch? This isn't cops and robbers, you know.'

'If you don't want to come I'll go alone.'

'I'm sure you would.' For the first time he was showing resentment, not ashamed of it now though he had it under a rigid control. He considered again, then decided quickly. He didn't want further complications, a public humiliation to add to the score of a private defeat, so it was better to go with Margaret if only to have a hand on the brake. In her present mood she might be stupider than Peter. 'All right,' he said, 'I'll come with you.'

They took a taxi to the Herengracht, dismissing it at the Utrechtsestraat bridge, then walking along the southern bank. Opposite von Frei's house they stopped. Margaret looked both ways and shook her head.

'He isn't here.'

'Of course he isn't." Laver was acid. 'Do you think he'd stand here openly for everyone in that house to see, making a perfect fool of himself as you and I are precisely doing? I don't know what his plan is but he won't just walk up to the house and knock.' He looked at the cabin cruiser. 'She's sailing this evening, I think you said.'

'So Peter thought.'

'Then whatever his plan I'd guess he'll time it for that. Meanwhile all he needs is observation and he can do that without our seeing him. From any of four corners and probably all. A quick glance—we shan't see him. In the intervals he'll move around, on foot or in a car perhaps. It's no good going after him, he'd see us and lose us easily, especially if he has a car.' Laver stopped himself suddenly. 'Car—'

'What are you thinking?'

'Nothing really but it's worth a check. De Masseys is in the Amstel, round the corner.' He looked at his watch. 'There'll be somebody there still. Wait.'

He came back in ten minutes and walking fast. 'Dinoba went in to borrow a car and they gave him one unquestioningly. An off-white Volkswagen.'

'With one arm?'

'According to what you told me the other one's out of a sling—he can use it.'

There were parked cars on both sides of the Herengracht and Margaret looked up and down again. 'Three Volkswagens but none of them white.'

'Of course not, he'll be moving around.' Richard read her thoughts from her anxious face. 'Just waste of time to look for him.'

He leant against the iron railing, watching. On and around

173   DD—M

the cruiser there was the air of a brisk activity. Men were bringing out stores, two sailors were loading them, a man in a gold-laced cap was giving the orders. 'You were right,' Richard said, 'she'll be leaving this evening.' He ran a landsman's eye down the white-painted vessel. 'I think she's ocean-going, comfortably. Sleep six or maybe seven, I'd say. Three crew but always one on watch. Room for four others.'

'Will Frei be going too, do you think?'

'I don't see why he should be unless he fancies the trip for pleasure. After all, he isn't a scientist.'

She said quietly: 'Peter was going, I'm sure of that.'

'And now he isn't. He can thank you for that whatever happens.'

'I don't want his thanks, I never did.'

He slid expertly off the dangerous ground. 'And Jacky?' he asked.

'Jacky's going all right and he won't come back. Why should they trouble to bring him back?'

She was speaking with cool indifference and he risked a sideways glance at her. 'Aren't you sorry for Jacky Dolan at all?' He didn't expect an affirmative answer.

'Not in the least, he asked for it. Going to my father like that, meaning to sell what the old man told him.'

'I am in a way, a little bit. I know he was an impostor but he wasn't an unattractive one. And when a man gets out of his league he's finished. Nemesis—there are lots of words.'

'I know several simpler English ones.'

He was silent, he couldn't scratch her shell. It was his instinct it wasn't as hard as she showed it but he wasn't the man to make the test. What had he said once to Martin Dominy? A man would have to be very sure.

A tender was chugging alongside the cruiser, passing a pipe which a seaman fastened. 'Fuelling-up,' Richard said. 'Dangerous in a canal like this, especially if it's petrol.'

'Paul Frei has this town sewn up in a bag.'

'I knew that when we talked to de Kuyper.' He was bitter now and she noticed it.

'You don't like him?'

'Why should I?'

'I liked him a lot and he gave me a present.'

'I could see you had a rug with you.'

'If it interests you it's worth a small fortune.'

'The man's a millionaire,' he said.

'He's a great deal more than a millionaire.' She'd been going to say something more but stopped, pointing instead at the pumping tender. The hose was still connected but the tender had edged much closer now. On the afterdeck of the cruiser men were loading on drums, lashing them down professionally.

'Extra petrol?' Margaret Seyer asked.

'I suppose so since it's come from the tender.'

'A longer trip than usual, then?'

'Or the avoidance of calls to take on fuel.' He looked at the forty-gallon drums. 'No smoking on that ship,' he said.

Frei's secretary had been amusing himself again with Jacky Dolan . . . The two other guests he'd spoken of had duly arrived from Germany and they'd all be leaving that evening . . . All of them? The question was sensible. So there would be Mr. Dolan, the two scientists from Germany, himself and a crew of three. Another guest had been intended but had been allowed to leave the house in circumstances which the secretary considered foolish in the extreme. He didn't mind telling Dolan this since it was unlikely he would repeat it to his employer. In fact it was more than unlikely, it was impossible. Mr. Dolan and Frei would never meet now since it really wouldn't be necessary. Ever.

As Jacky's face fell to pieces the secretary sneered again.

He was confident the trip would be a pleasant one. The ship was well-found, the crew well-trained. The captain would naturally navigate, and one of the men was a very fair cook while the other had, well, had special skills. Very special skills. And they weren't going through the North Sea Canal, they were going into the Zuider Zee. A most interesting area with all those new polders. Rather lonely, though, and there were treacherous currents. It was notoriously dangerous for unwise bathing. People who couldn't swim very well were always getting drowned off yachts. There'd been four or five last summer, and though one shouldn't bet on certainties the secretary was ready to wager that there was bound to be at least one this year.

Jacky didn't take all of it in. He was utterly broken, almost uncaring. When the doctor arrived he didn't resist. The doctor gave him a crushing sedative.

Laver was leaning on the fine railing still and watching. He had known the Executive wasn't omnipotent but he hadn't expected he'd ever feel quite so helpless. Would Charles Russell have been ineffective too? Yes, if he'd been standing here now, but the point was he never would have been. That wasn't his form, to be pushed into corners; he'd have known ways and means to force that Dutchman's reluctant hand, and as for Margaret Seyer he'd have known perfectly how to control her, even how to turn her into an asset which he could use. Charles Russell had years of experience, Richard none. He'd been treated as a lightweight and was conscious that was his rating still.

He watched on with Margaret Seyer, uneasy. Looking at it sensibly there was nothing Peter Dinoba could do. He hadn't a weapon and couldn't get one, for this wasn't a town which sold firearms across the counter. So come raving along and make a scene? He was welcome to that, they'd soon suppress him. No doubt it would be an embarrassment, but regarded as serious mischief-maker it was hard to take Peter seriously. Yet he'd borrowed a car which didn't fit. He wouldn't need one to keep a watch on this house, which suggested he had some other plan, that he might not be coming here at all. It was impossible to read that mind, an African in extreme emotion. He had reason to be in extreme emotion, but that made the uncertainty worse, the man more dangerous.

Activity round the cruiser was building up. The tender was stowing her hose and backing away, the seamen had finished lashing the fuel drums. Down the steps of Frei's house walked two men in black overcoats. Both carried briefcases, one a small box. Richard said: 'Boffins,' perfectly sure of it. They hadn't the air of Englishmen but the type was unmistakable. They went down the ladder and into the cabin.

Margaret had been watching too and nodded a brief agreement. 'Two scientists and the crew,' she said. 'That's one to come.'

In fact there were two and they were making their way down the nearer of two flights of steps. Jacky D had an arm round the other man's shoulders, evidently not fully conscious but equally not quite unconscious either, moving his feet in a ragged drugged dream. Margaret said: 'That's the secretary—I met him,' falling again into watchful silence. The two men came on unsteadily, crossing the road between house and canal then, helped by a sailor, down a ladder into the cockpit between the cabin and the afterdeck. There were benches here and both sat down. Jacky's head fell on his chest at once and the secretary stayed there guarding him.

Richard Laver was sensing the crisis now. If Dinoba was going to act all all he'd have to pull it soon or never. He looked up the canal and down again, at the four nearest corners where two bridges crossed the water. From any of these Dinoba could see though it was certain he wasn't positioned there. He'd use them in turn for a look perhaps, then keep changing, secure in movement. That way . . .

He had a sudden and fleeting snapshot impression of a man who'd appeared on one corner and gone. It was too far away to see his face and he'd come, turned and run in a single movement.

The bustle around the cruiser was working steadily to its climax, the last luggage brought out from the house and stowed, the mooring ropes cast off and coiled, the ladder pulled in, the twin engines growling. Richard Laver, the landsman, watched with interest, recognizing what was a ritual just as much as it was an effective drill. In the wheelhouse forward the captain spun the wheel to port and the starboard screw went Half Ahead.

Richard felt Margaret's fingers bite his arm. She was gesturing with her other hand and he looked where her rigid arm was pointing. On the road on the other side was a car, an off-white Volkswagen driving fast. The driver had her in second still and the engine was howling noisily. Where the cruiser had moored, the canal-rail had been taken down and the driver had almost reached the gap. He banged his right hand down and slammed the brakes, getting his skid as he changed again expertly. Now the car was facing the gap and the water. The driver gunned the engine and the car went over the edge accelerating. Its nose dipped at once and fell accurately into the cockpit. One man had started to move but had moved too late, the other hadn't even tried. The crash came brutally clearly, more than gravity behind the fall. The Volkswagen teetered, then settled sideways. There'd been a single scream of terror, then total silence.

Margaret started to run but Richard held her. She struggled; he pulled her down. 'There's nothing you can do, nor I. There's a hundred gallons of fuel at least in those drums they've got on the afterdeck, and in the main tanks forward God knows what. If that car catches fire it'll wreck the block.'

She lay quiet for a second, perhaps waiting for it as he was. Then she began to struggle again.

'Keep down—running's crazy. It's sixty yards to the nearest corner, and if the blast catches us on our feet . . . Flying glass . . .'

'I've got to get down there to him.'

He held her the tighter but raised his head . . . Think what you liked of seamen's ritual but undeniably they knew their drill. A klaxon was blaring urgently and already they had the extinguishers out. The car was almost submerged in foam and the tender was moving in again, her own much more powerful fire-jet playing. Soon the Volkswagen was invisible.

Richard Laver got up and Margaret with him. He stared at the mass of foam, said quietly: 'Whoever's inside that wreck won't burn.'

'And underneath it?'

'I'm afraid there won't be a great deal left. Not with a seven-foot fall at that pace.'

'It was Jacky and that secretary?'

'You saw them too.'

They had started to move but stopped again as a sailor began to scoop at the foam, working on the Volkswagen's door. It had jammed but he used a crowbar, bursting it open from fragile hinges, helping the man who crawled out unsteadily. He was shaken but he seemed to be whole. Then a seaman took each of his arms and held him.

They began to walk him towards the house but halted. A big man had come out of it, had looked once at the wreck and now stood in the roadway. He spoke to the sailors curtly. They looked surprised but dropped Peter's arms. The big man said clearly:

'Be off with you.'

Peter Dinoba stared at him.

'Be off. The police will want to talk to you—I don't. You've done what you wanted to do. Congratulations.' Frei returned to the sailors, changing to German. 'Get a crane and an ambulance. There won't be a lot for the latter to do.'

He went back into the house again. He'd said all that he needed to say, he'd given his orders.

Peter Dinoba began to walk, along the canal, across the bridge, straight at Richard and Margaret Seyer. At first he didn't see them, then he did. He hesitated but came on steadily.

Margaret said: 'Peter—'

He didn't answer. His face as he passed her was frozen in hate. For an instant her own collapsed, then she shrugged. She said to Richard Laver softly:

'So he isn't for me and he never was.'

17

Richard Laver had postponed his flight to London, and next day was calling on de Kuyper again, this time at the Commissioner's request. The difference in his reception had been remarkable. Today de Kuyper was co-operation personified, *cher collègue* to the edge of parody. Whatever his first opinion of him Richard would always have conceded that he'd been frank, and this morning he was both frank and helpful. His difficulties, he said at once, had been removed by a single telephone call. It had come from Paul von Frei in person who had made his, well, his preferences plain. Since they were sensible, sound administratively, the Commissioner had had no difficulty in falling in with them at once. Since they were sensible, sound administratively, he had equally no doubt whatever that Mr. Laver would find them acceptable too. As the Commissioner's friends the police already had.

The Commissioner poured the ritual gin . . . So let us start at the beginning. If he'd been understanding Mr. Laver correctly, then the Security Executive had been worried about something called Selective Pigmentation Disease, and in particular it had been worried that one Dolan had known too much of it and had come to Amsterdam to sell his knowledge. Which might or might not be correct—that wasn't Dutch business as he'd once been obliged to make brutally clear. But Dolan was now dead, and all the circumstances suggested that his knowledge had perished with him. Since they could now speak freely as the colleagues they were, it was de Kuyper's firm opinion that there'd been nobody in Paul Frei's house capable of evaluating a matter of such advanced microbiology: on the contrary two gentlemen from Germany with letters after their names by the inch had arrived a few hours before the, er, accident. Which had prevented a cruise in the Zuider Zee, which in turn might well have been fruitful to the two scientists. All this no doubt was theory, but it was supported by Paul Frei's subsequent actions. If he'd in fact had designs on S.P.D. and on Dolan who bore the knowledge of it, it was significant that on Dolan's death he'd apparently cut his losses promptly, a typical decision by your genuine copper-bottomed tycoon who never flogged failing horses to death. So Paul Frei had gone on a holiday, leaving the city that morning to stay at a clinic. He'd said he'd be away three weeks and he hoped to lose three stone at least.

The Commissioner poured more gin; he was clearly happy . . . Not that this deplorable germ mightn't still present problems for Richard Laver, but they'd be problems where they belonged, in England, and since de Kuyper was speaking frankly again he was delighted that they should remain there. And of course there was Peter Dinoba still, but tycoons had other powers and strengths than a willingness to cut their losses. For instance they hated the police around; they hated all kinds of fuss and bother, complications which wasted their time and showed no profit. In the matter of Peter Dinoba, Paul von Frei had again been helpful.

The Dutchman stared at Richard Laver . . . There'd been some trouble in England, hadn't there? A man found dead whom Dinoba had known, and the fact that Dinoba had come here wounded. A single fingerprint would clinch such a case, but the Commissioner's information was that the gun had belonged to the man who was dead. A cast-iron answer of self-defence, any competent lawyer could handle it intoxicated. The Commissioner had smiled knowingly. And had not British judges a well-known complex about fire-arms? It was true the dead man had been strangled to death, but he'd pulled a gun and shot his strangler, and if one happened to hold a throat just too long when its owner was firing a gun and had wounded you . . .

However all that was Laver's business if indeed he found intervention necessary. It would all take place in England again when Peter Dinoba returned there. Which in fact would be in a matter of minutes since he'd been put on a plane an hour ago.

Richard started to speak but de Kuyper held a hand up. No, he hadn't been deported and there'd been nothing done officially: on the contrary he'd gone of his own free will and glad of the chance to do so. Naturally there'd been arrangements first, certain undertakings both asked and given. Paul Frei had been very reasonable. There'd been an accident, he'd insisted on that, and when Paul Frei insisted officials listened. So there'd been a shocking piece of driving and alas two men had died in it. That couldn't be wholly smothered but nor was there need to try to. There would have to be an inquiry, but Dinoba wasn't a casual tourist; he was employed by de Masseys who weighed heavily in Amsterdam, he was a respectable man in a fine position and no doubt he'd continue to keep it now. He came to this city frequently, so he wouldn't have to be extradited on some capital charge which might risk his future. No, he'd return here perfectly freely to face an inquiry and possibly a process too. If the court got really nasty he might conceivably earn a suspended sentence but a swingeing fine was much more likely. After all he was a de Masseys man and de Masseys, like Paul Frei, were powerful. That was the way it went and why complain?

The Commissioner poured a third shot of gin . . . So Paul Frei had been co-operative but of course he'd wanted a *quid pro quo*. Dinoba, very sensibly, had given it. There'd been an extraordinary affair of some coloured man snatched from a boat-cruise at night and the police were still inquiring about it. They would inquire for a decent time and then close the file. It had been darkening on the water, and this wasn't a town where a coloured man was noticed as a rarity. Dinoba could return here safely since it was very unlikely he'd ever be recognized. In any case most of that boatload had been tourists. So one coloured man had driven carelessly and another had been kidnapped by force. There was nothing to connect the two but a statement by either there'd only been one. That statement would not be forthcoming, now or ever. Very wisely indeed, de Kuyper thought. If Paul Frei had taken a different view a charge of murder was very serious. Dinoba had made a very good bargain. So had Frei, in his manner, who hated fusses, fusses with policemen and lawyers especially.

The Commissioner rose and held out his hand. *Au revoir, cher collègue.* Till our next pleasant meeting.

Richard Laver decided that he'd walk to Margaret Seyer's hotel. He enjoyed Dutch gin but had an adequate experience of it, and at an advertised thirty-five per cent it could be almost as lethal as vodka. He was in excellent humour, his anger forgotten. She'd treated him quite outrageously but she wouldn't be conscious she'd done anything extraordinary. You took women as God had made them if you wished to live with them fruitfully, thanking Him if you felt like it that the mould for the Margaret Seyers was seldom used. In any case brewing resentment was stupid. Tolerance could be taken too far, but resentment was, above all things, frustrating, it carried you nowhere and dulled the sun.

He was shown into a sitting room and Margaret was standing to greet him. It surprised him that she'd taken two rooms and she read his mind if not his face.

'You're thinking I'm splashing the money a bit?'

'None of my business,' he said politely.

'If it interests you in any way this isn't where I slept last night.'

'Indeed?' He could see that she meant to tell him.

'I went down to pay my bill this morning and there wasn't a bill for me to pay. Instead there was this suite, if you call it that. Entirely at my disposal for twenty-one days. No message—nothing. Nobody will say a word.'

He looked round the room, much more than interested. There were fresh roses in a vase, magnificent blooms. 'Two dozen red roses,' he said. He was quoting.

'No, I've counted them. There are twenty-one.'

. . . Three weeks and twenty-one roses, twenty-one days. It was delicate, very un-German. Just a flower a day. Twenty-one, if you happened to think of it, was also the half of forty-two. Twenty-one pounds was half three stone. That was two pounds a day, a killing schedule. All right for the first few days perhaps, but it was the last ten pounds which defeated you. Richard Laver smiled. They wouldn't defeat Paul Frei if he meant to lose them.

'Would you like a drink?' she was asking him, already at a wall cupboard. Inside was a rack of wine and a small refrigerator. 'I think champagne might be appropriate.'

'To hell with being appropriate. I like it.'

'You're not alone in that,' she said.

'I'm not?' It was very good wine and went well after gin. 'He's doing you very nicely indeed.'

'There's a car as well and a man to drive it. No money, of course.'

'There wouldn't be if I'm guessing right.'

Another woman might have giggled but Margaret laughed. 'I don't suppose I'll need much like this.'

'And you haven't an idea—'

'I haven't.'

'You're a liar,' he said pleasantly.

'All right, I'm a liar.' She was looking extremely well, he thought, five years younger and quietly glowing.

'And will you stay here for the period offered?' He saw that a rug had been laid out prominently. He knew little about them technically but knew superlative work when he saw it.

'I haven't made up my mind but it's certainly interesting.'

'And your father?'

'I'm ringing him twice a day at least. He's happy, he doesn't need me now.'

'You like this town?'

'I always have.'

'And its inhabitants?'

'I like one of them very much indeed.'

As he rose to go she put a hand on his arm; she was suddenly very serious. 'Will you tell me one thing, Richard, please?'

'I will if I know the answer.'

'Do you think I'd make a good rich man's wife?'

'You'd make a marvellous wife to any man provided he could scare you stiff.'

'Yes,' she said happily, 'that's the point. You're even smarter than I thought you were. You must come to the wedding supposing there is one.'

'Expect me in three weeks precisely.'

Richard walked back to his hotel for his bag, then took a taxi to the Museumplein. He had an hour to kill before the afternoon flight, and though he'd missed his lunch he wasn't hungry. He wasn't drunk or anywhere near it but was aware that he had taken wine. Champagne after that Dutchman's gin—at his age he should know better than that.

Nevertheless he didn't regret it. He had intended to see the Vermeers again but decided to stay in the open air. He chose a bench in the pale Dutch sunshine, feeling the glow of a mild euphoria. Richard Laver's first case, he thought again: it hadn't been a distinguished one but by God he'd had beginner's luck. He needn't offer his resignation now, the affair had turned out by the book in the end. The intransitive mood was emphatically right: no virtue of Richard Laver's that it hadn't just ended in total disaster. Beginner's luck and he'd needed it.

So everything was fine, or was it? Laver was conscious the drink was dying, the mild euphoria fading with the rare sun. Selective Pigmentation Disease . . .

It was there still, it existed. Ministers, since it hadn't leaked, could play on at their incomprehensible games, and on Open Days at that Wiltshire Establishment you could walk around perfectly freely. They'd show you the people catching colds, the latest protective clothing, anything. Anything they could call Defence.

And no doubt they'd also insist that you knew that it hadn't been many years ago that one of their own men had died of plague, that in a simulated attack a few months ago a harmless agent had been sprayed off the east coast of England, effectively blanketing all the south below a line from the Wash to Birmingham. And of course if you called on a non-open day they'd show you round just as blandly. Particularly if you happened to add that you were a professional microbiologist.

Richard Laver rose and began to walk. What had one of their own seniors called it? Biological warfare—the bargain basement for mass destruction. Sooner or later some small country with a couple of good microbiologists and a hate against another . . . That might be contained and possibly could be, but S.P.D. was different in kind. Selective. In a sense that Establishment wasn't important, since this wouldn't be the first time that the break had come in England whilst the real resources, the power to develop, lay well to the west and east of a Wiltshire down. There were areas of the world which would be happier and more prosperous if their inhabitants were ruthlessly halved, but much more frightening than that forgivable thought there were towns and even countries where citizens of one colour would secretly breathe a sigh of relief if citizens of another were simply not there. Richard remembered a figure exactly for it had scared him more than battle had. Nine million, two hundred and eighty-nine thousand, eight hundred and ten human beings, presumably sane, had recently gone to their polling booths and voted for an insanity.

He found he was outside a church and on an impulse went into it quickly. It was a Catholic church but he knew the drill. He put a ten guilder note in the proper box, taking the appropriate candle, looking for an image of Saint Anthony of Padua. He remembered his father had called them idols. He'd once owned a Venetian girl friend and she'd explained about Saint Anthony. He was the only world-class saint of the Veneto, the only one worth a serious investment like ten guilders. Richard had discovered that she prayed to the saint not through him and had told her that this was heretical. One would say anything when one was really young. The lady had been horrified and had dropped him for a waiter. The waiter had been a good Catholic and hadn't cared a button for doctrine.

Richard didn't find his statue but a tolerable painting instead. He lit his candle from another, bowing formally to Saint Anthony. He stuck the candle on a spike and knelt.

He said the Lord's Prayer. It was all he could remember.